D1218453

THE COLD HARD LIGHT

THE
COLD
HARD
LIGHT

CHRISTOPHER AMENTA

**BLACK
STONE**
PUBLISHING

Copyright © 2022 by Christopher Amenta
Published in 2022 by Blackstone Publishing
Cover design by Gunjan Ahlawat

The characters and events in this book are fictitious.
Any similarity to real persons, living or dead, is coincidental
and not intended by the author.

Printed in the United States of America

First edition: 2022
ISBN 979-8-200-70501-6
Fiction / Literary

Version 2

CIP data for this book is available
from the Library of Congress

Blackstone Publishing
31 Mistletoe Rd.
Ashland, OR 97520

www.BlackstonePublishing.com

To my parents

ONE

Here's how come H fought: for that moment when the instinct to take a beating like so much medicine gave in to one that told him to survive. Isn't that something? Turns out we want to live.

As soon as the giant was on him, H felt this fuse light. He tossed his gloves to the ice, squared his skates, dropped his helmet, and up came both fists, knotted now, knuckled, as if a grenade had been plunked onto the end of each wrist. Pull the pin and see what. Half a minute passed with them turning around each other, eyeing, waiting. The rink quieted. Patience, huh, was the virtue. Just before, the big guy offered a grin, a crooked thing that was short about a dozen teeth, and H knew the type. These bruisers enjoyed a lifetime of free orthodontia courtesy of one team's fighter or the next. They took and gave punches like the rest of us opened mail. The skulls on these guys, one callous at a time, had hardened into something like steel: a shell to protect the shell. They hurtled fists like heaving cannonballs. Yours glanced off without so much as a sound.

This guy gave that smile and H knew. Here came trouble.

Here came pain. Once again, H had misjudged. Once again, he would get his due. Too late, though. Look left, look right, and H was the only one standing there. These referees backed away and let all takers go. They weren't anybody's papas.

H dug his skates into the ice. A fight like this turned on balance, on counterstrike. Even the biggest guys could be pulled from their marks. All that weight and power could be used against them. H took hold of the guy's shoulder pads, clutched a handful of jersey, and yanked to stoop the man, to put the guy's face into that spot where a punch, once thrown, would be climbing, rising, ready to leave the atmosphere.

H thought, Every fight is a long shot. He thought, Every fight has two losers. And then he felt something like a railroad tie come hammering across his left ear.

Adrenaline like a magic eraser, and the next thing H saw was the ceiling of their locker room. He blinked. His eyes focused and his sight returned. He was lying on his back, looking up.

Overhead, the light fixture swayed as the crowd above, now bloodthirsty and fevered, stamped their boots on the bleachers. How they love a fight. Listen to them bay. Put any one of them on the ice, though, and watch them scamper. Ours, H thought, is a nation of spectators. We've no judges or teachers, doctors or priests. Everywhere he looked he saw critics.

H tasted blood—metallic, salty. The stadium settled. Soon the ringing in his ears dulled, then subsided, and he heard the sound of a whistle chirping, of cheers hushing as the game began again. Glad to hear, he thought, that his pain could amuse. His knuckles felt shattered. He counted his teeth with his tongue. Crotch, heartbeat, both eyes, ten fingers, ten toes, anyway, H was still whole.

The door opened and somebody came into the locker room, but H couldn't muster the energy to turn his head. He kept watching the ceiling. One of the guys had brought the rest of his gear down, he thought, or maybe the trainer wanted to kick around his tires and make sure the engine still worked. Instead, though, as H watched the light above him flicker, his uncle's face, gray and morose, came dangling, upside down, into view.

"Pick a hand," Billy said.

H's head throbbed. He squinted to focus his vision. "You can't be in here."

"Go ahead," Billy said. "Pick one."

Billy had tucked both hands behind his back, out of sight, and leaning forward, he shimmied his shoulders in a gesture that seemed to threaten his balance.

Because H didn't want the guy to fall over, he sat up, turned to him, and said, "Left."

Billy produced the right and offered a clump of snow that he must have taken from the Zamboni garage. He kept the other hand twisted behind him.

"That big fellow treated your head like a dog on a fire hydrant. Your face worked like a buffet for his fists."

H took the snow and pressed it to his cheek. It burned cold, and as it melted, water trickled along his jaw, down the line of his neck, to the plane of his chest.

"I got a few shots in," he said.

Billy, still hiding one hand, took and unfolded a metal chair from against the door to the showers and sat. His trousers lifted, revealing shins and legs that seemed too thin to support his frame. Even seated the man looked unsteady.

Billy folded his free arm over his belly, crumpled his face along his eyes, tilted his head, and pursed his lips.

H took the ice from his cheek. His knuckles, red and bloodied, throbbed, and he lifted the wound for Billy to see. "What's this if I got whipped so bad?"

Billy leaned forward to make a show of inspecting H's hand. "I'm no doctor."

"Absolutely you're not."

"I'm no forensic scientist, but in that mess, I wouldn't be surprised if you landed a few shots on your own face. You were all spun about. I wouldn't be shocked to learn that you could no longer name your presidents, if you couldn't count backward from one."

H stood and tossed the snow, which slopped to the rubber floor and began to melt pink. He sat in his cubby, stripped away his jersey and his shoulder pads, and started unlacing his skates. "Like I told you, you can't be in here."

"Let me guess what Coach said."

"How'd you even get down here? There's supposed to be a guy at the end of the hall."

"He said, 'Quit fighting,' didn't he? He told you, 'It does nobody any good.'"

"My head hurts, Billy."

"That man has no vision. Zero. Nada. He couldn't piece a game together with a roster full of Olympians."

"Maybe fuck off, Billy. Maybe stop coming to my games. You got any sense of what it means to be unwelcome?"

"I'm the mayor of that city," Billy said. "I'm ground zero for being unwanted. You know that."

Billy's belly slumped against his shirt. He took his hat from his head and hooked it onto his knee. A chunk of bangs fell forward onto his face. His hair had thinned since H had seen him last. A patch of skin shimmered around the top of his skull. H thought of a sheet of ice after the Zamboni runs: perfect, unspoiled. The man had a few days' growth on his cheeks and breath so foul that H thought he could see it.

Billy leaned forward. "Anyway, pick a hand."

H kicked off one skate and started loosening the other.

"H," Billy said. "Do you think this is the only thing I've got to do today?"

"You act like I asked you to come interfere with my life." H unlatched the belt of his pants. "I pick a hand, and you'll leave?"

"Like I never was, son. Like a happy dream you can't remember come morning."

"All right. What is it? What, Billy, is it that you want?"

Billy produced his left hand, in which he held a brown paper bag—a sandwich bag—which he offered to H. "For you," he said.

H hammered the heel of each skate against the floor. He ran his thumb and his forefinger down both sides of both blades to clean away the snow, then dried the metal with a towel he kept in his locker. "What's this?" he said.

Billy rocked the bag. The paper crinkled. Billy made both eyebrows jump. Once upon a time, they'd played this game with butterscotch candies, with silver dollar coins.

H stopped undressing and opened the package. Inside was a gun: an ugly, snub-nosed thing about which H knew nothing except that it looked like something he'd seen detectives spin and fire in old noir movies. Outside of a cop's holster or the display case at a sporting goods store, he'd never seen a gun, never held, pointed, or shot one. His temples throbbed. He seemed able to feel blood pulsing through him, reddening the irises of his eyes, thudding from chest to forearms to fingers.

"Jesus," H said. "What do I want this for?" H turned the top of the bag closed and jammed the package back into Billy's gut, maybe harder than he'd meant to. Billy started coughing.

"You lunatic," H said. "Go home. Get sober. Stop coming here."

For a while, Billy just coughed and wheezed, but then his breathing settled, and he took his hat from his knee and, clutching the package, stood. He combed his hair with his hand, turned toward the door, then turned back.

"Where is it you think all this is going, kid?" Billy spread out his arms. "What are you, twenty-three, twenty-four? A minor-league player with minor-league moves. Driving a cab around at night for businessmen and businesswomen and all their toothy, rich kids. You haven't got a friend in the world, and you don't deserve one, anyway. You've got no money, a piece of shit car, half an education, and zero future."

"Not that it's any of your business, but scouts come to these games all the time."

"Wonderful," Billy said. "Let's hope one of them's looking for a punching bag. Let's hope that some triple-A squad needs a face to get trampled each week. It'd sell tickets, anyway." He shook his head. "Quit dreaming, kid. If it was going to happen, it would've. Grow up. Stop moping. Stop acting like not making the NHL is something to be ashamed of."

H turned again to his equipment. He unfastened his shin pads, pulled off both socks and his pants, the jock next, and then his shorts. He stood and wrapped himself in a towel. "It'd be a terrific favor to us all if you'd wander off somewhere and finally die," H said, digging a bottle of shampoo from his bag. "Don't you think you've done enough?"

Billy started pacing, and his trench coat stormed around his knees. Then he stopped. "There's another option, H."

H stepped into a pair of flip-flops. "I have to shower."

"You and me, we both got a raw deal. You and me both don't deserve this ending. We've spent the last ten years shuffling around feeling sorry for ourselves. What's enough? Did it ever occur to you that just because you feel like a loser doesn't mean that you are one? That losing all your life is as much a choice as it is a lousy stretch of luck?"

"I'm tired, Billy." H turned his cheek into the light and touched the bruise on his face. "See this? Believe it or not, it hurts."

Billy pointed two fingers—index, middle—of his right hand at H. "You had all the potential in the world. You know that? Your dad wanted you to be a doctor. Your mom thought you'd be a teacher because of how much you liked your schoolwork. There was even a time when I believed this hockey business would go for you. You had eyes for the game. Even Sarah—"

"Let's not talk about her."

"Sarah—"

"That's enough."

"H," Billy said, sitting. "How long do you plan to go on hiding?"

H put his back to his uncle and walked toward the showers. "Goodbye, Billy. Stop coming here, would you?"

"He's out," Billy said.

H paused. The game clock rounded the three-minute mark.

"Williams," Billy said.

"Bullshit."

"Eleven years, H. Did you think they were going to keep to him forever?"

H turned. His uncle clutched his hat to his chest as if pledging to a flag. His eyes, now folded into the bridge of his nose, were drooped and wet.

"Your kid—H, you've got a kid now. That's a blessing. So maybe things have changed. Maybe now your hockey only goes so far. That's not losing, H. That's not game over. Wake up. Take a breath. There's bigger fish frying. You've got a bloodline, H." He knocked his knuckles against his chest. "We've got a bloodline. Which means that we've got something to live for. That girl is what matters now, H. Your little girl."

"That's right."

"So live, already. Take the gun. Be a man. Stand up for yourself. End this thing, correctly, please. Then, tuck in your shirttail and comb your hair and get on living. For your daughter, H—for my grandniece. Don't you think she deserves that?"

"Jesus." H touched the scruff on his chin. "Eleven years."

A horn sounded. The crowd above them cheered. Boots stamped on bleachers. The duct work rattled. Somebody had scored. The game clock on the wall paused at 2:03. "Hear that?" Billy said. "Your boys just added the go-ahead."

"Them or us?"

Billy shook his head. "Listen to the crowd. You know

perfectly well." Billy pointed to H's hand. "You and I know what part you played. I see your sacrifice. Shame on them for ignoring it."

"I've got to shower, Billy."

"You were raised by babes when wolves is what you needed. I see you, son." Billy tapped his temple. "I'm standing right here."

Billy raised the sandwich bag in his hand, cocked the bundle to the left, once, then back. He stood and walked over to H's locker and placed the package inside the boot of H's skate.

"Put a bow on the thing, huh?" Billy said. "It's not going to be me. I'm too old for any kind of redemption. My play is to slowly drink myself to death. I'm working on it. But you?" He put those two fingers to H's chest. "You've still got something left in the tank. There's a life to be had for a kid like you—if you want it."

H felt a stab of pity, an urge to offer the man a shoulder or a hand. He said nothing. The bruises on his face felt ablaze. "Fuck, Billy. Honestly, what's any of this to you?"

Billy returned his hat to his crown and smiled. The horn sounded. The game had ended. Billy moved toward the door.

"Believe it or not, I'm rooting for you. Wrap it up, son." He pointed to the ceiling. "Not much time now, hmm?"

He jerked his head toward the wall. H, following the gesture, saw the top of the bag inside the boot of his skate.

When he turned back, Billy had gone, and the door, on its double hinge, feathered shut behind him. When it swung open again, the guys came in, red-faced with steam rising from their skin. H gave them his back and went to shower.

TWO

The moment H walked into the apartment, Christine handed him the baby.

"Here," she said, and she held Jo by the armpits, belly out, like passing a sack of groceries.

"Welcome home," H said. Shifting his hockey sticks to his right hand, he gathered his daughter in his left and became aware, then, of the gun still in the bag in his pants pocket. He imagined it alight, glowing like a beacon. He imagined it bursting into flames.

"Welcome home," Christine said, and then, unburdened, she ducked into the bedroom, tying her hair up into a ponytail, the hood of her sweatshirt swishing as she went.

"Welcome home," H said again to himself. He leaned his sticks against the refrigerator, then lifted and turned his daughter so they faced one another. "You miss me, kid?"

Spit bubbled from the girl's lips.

"Want to hear how I did tonight?" he asked the baby.

Jo squirmed in his arms and turned toward the sounds

coming from the bedroom. Christine couldn't get far enough from Jo, but all the girl ever wanted was her mother.

"You and everybody else," H told her, and then he put the kid in her high chair and lowered the tray before her chest. "Anything to eat?" he called to Christine.

"I'm going swimming," she said from the other room.

"Is there any dinner?"

Christine leaned into the doorframe. She'd already changed into her Speedo and a pair of sweatpants. The spandex flattened the paunch that she wanted so furiously to disappear, and in the suit, she reminded him of the kid she'd once been who served him quesadillas and Mexican beers and had laughed at everything he said and had left him her phone number on the receipt. "Call me," she'd written. Arms dangling above her, belly cinched, she recalled that girl from a pregnancy ago, a few years and a pregnancy, and all the madness in between, like déjà vu, like a trance replacing the air in the room with story.

The feeling passed.

"I've been watching her all day," Christine said, pulling the rings from her fingers. "H, I've had her all day." She disappeared into the bedroom again to place the jewelry in a tray she kept on top of her dresser.

The clock on the microwave read 10:13, which meant that it was 10:04. "What'd you eat?"

From the bedroom, she said, "Popcorn."

H rubbed his chin, wondering if what fed the mother fed the baby. You are what you eat. Your kid is what her mother eats. H was heaving sandbags atop a levy. He was plugging leaks with his fingers. He looked at the child. "Is that all you had tonight? Popcorn?"

Jo gave him eyes like parachutes deploying, which made H smile. Go swimming there, Christine, he wanted to say. Be like every other mother on the planet and dive right in there, please.

"What a hurricane you've come into, little one. What a time to be alive." He touched the baby's cheek. "Better toughen up. Better put scales on that skin, huh? It's shells and mortars from day one."

He turned from his daughter and looked around the room until he decided: the gun, still in its bag, went underneath the couch cushion. He'd find some way to toss it later. H sat and, shifting his weight around, tried to find any sense of the thing beneath him, which he couldn't. Christine was in the other room hammering through her routine. Her getting ready sounded like a highway construction zone. Seemed as though the rule went that she had to drop everything once—her bag, her hair straightener, her wallet, her phone—before she could put it all where it went and be ready to go.

"Can a girl live on popcorn?" he asked Christine.

She came from the room and put her bag on the kitchen table. There, a fern sat shriveled and yellowed in its clay pot, seeming to produce more stench than it absorbed, which had been Christine's point for the thing to begin with. H filled a glass at the sink, drank half, and poured the rest over the plant. Water pooled atop the soil. Seemed cruel, he thought, that you could somehow starve and drown a plant all at once. He looked at the baby. How many things might go wrong? How many ways to fail? Dog eat dog eat dog.

Christine started rooting around under her magazines and stacks of weeks-old mail, looking for her car keys.

"I said, why don't I make something?"

"The pool closes at midnight."

"Let's put some meat back on those bones," H said. "Let's put you back together again."

"This is my thing, H. You have your things. I don't interfere with your things."

"You're a giver."

"I'm in training. I wish you'd take it seriously. Besides, I've been cooped up in this house all day." She gave up looking and zipped shut the gym bag. "Can I have your keys?"

He nodded, produced them from his pocket, and placed them on the table, he realized, so that she'd have to come take them. When had nastiness become the ready response? Ashamed, he turned and went to the fridge. Anyway, how could you tell this woman a thing? She set a course like a railroad operator: straight lines and planned stops. The best a guy could do was sidle up alongside the tracks like a herd of cows and watch the show go thundering past. They never had a bite of fucking food to eat.

Jo gurgled.

"Did she have anything?" H took a package of eggs from the fridge and set them on the counter. His girl pressed her palms down on her tray, giggled, seemed amazed that those fingers were her own and that they moved when and how she told them to. Would he give up the girl to take her place and start all over again? He felt dizzy.

"What sort of mother do you think I am?"

H clicked on the burner and set a pan over the fire. There were no bowls in the cupboard, none drying on the rack. He took three eggs from the carton, set them loose on the stovetop, and returned the rest to the fridge. He could tell without looking over his shoulder that Christine was watching him, waiting for his response. H left the bait.

"I'll be home in an hour or so," she said, shouldering the bag.

"Listen."

"I have to go."

"Listen," he said again, but then he felt he didn't want to say anything at all. And he felt that some things weren't said straight away. Sometimes a guy sat down on a secret even though he knew he'd talk about it at some point, even though he knew that talking to a girlfriend, say, a partner, someone who'd always been both, would help, even though he knew that talking would stop a woman dead in her tracks and bring her back to Earth. Sometimes a guy said nothing, though speaking would be best, would be easy: "The guy that raped my sister is out of prison," he could say. "The guy that assaulted Sarah is walking free, and Uncle Billy wants him killed." "Benjamin Williams is out, and old Billy thinks I should shoot the guy dead." How about that?

Or, H thought, he could start the conversation with "Help." They could start there.

He laughed at the idea.

"What's funny?" she asked, then she turned to look at him for once. "Shit," she said. "Your face."

Christine dropped her bag, and the sound of gear slapping to linoleum startled the baby, who went quiet and trained those showstoppers on the floor.

"It's okay," H said, turning away.

She got him by the chin, tightly, but also somehow gently, and he thought, Of course she's a wonderful mother. Of course. How could I have doubted her? Why couldn't she have been mine?

She turned his face toward the light, toward her own, so she could study the shiner forming and the cut along his jaw. Still holding him, she brought her other hand forward and drew her fingertips along the wounds. H felt them like a salve.

"Why, honey?"

"It's all right," he said.

"Why don't you just stop? Why not cut yourself a break?"

"I'm fine, Christine," he said. "I'm just playing the game."

She shook her head. "No," she said. "That's not so. You and I both know that. Your girls need you whole. We want you in one piece." She took his hands. "Unclench these," she said. "Won't you? It'd be so easy."

She stepped toward him, and the first kiss she placed on his neck, as if afraid to go any closer. He curled around it, dipped his head, and felt drawn in for the next, which she deposited on his chin, and then for the one and the next that she placed on the bones around his eye socket.

His arms hung. He stooped.

"Billy came," he said into her hair.

He felt her fingernails on the back of his neck, circling the knobs of his spine.

"What did he want?" she said. "What could that old drunk possibly want?"

H nestled his forehead into the nape of her neck. "Just to haunt me. Only to never let me alone."

"Look here." She leaned back and took him by both cheeks and regarded him. "Look at me. We're your family now—me and Jo. That's right, isn't it?"

"We were close once," H said. "Once, during all that nonsense, Billy was my friend. He has a right to that, doesn't he?"

She embraced him again. "If you keep stretching in all directions at once, H, we'll never get you back into shape." Her voice softened. "I'm going to stay home tonight." She was writing letters with her fingernails on the skin below his hairline. Once, he'd been fluent in this language. "You and me," she said.

"No," H said, shaking his head.

"You and me and baby."

"No, that's not fair."

"Don't I get to decide?"

He stepped away from her. H looked at Jo and then at Christine. Then H looked at the couch cushion. "You'll miss the pool," he said.

"It'll be there tomorrow."

On the stove, oil started burning. Smoke lifted from the pan and rose toward the vent hood. H went and lowered the heat. "This is your thing," he said. "I don't want to keep you from it. Come home when you're done."

H cracked three eggs, tossed the shells into the sink, and broke the yolks with a fork. She came and hugged his back, and then she retrieved the gym bag and left. And when the door had closed, H turned from the stove and went and lifted the cushion and opened the bag, looked at his baby, and then looked at the gun. Jo cried out, and he put the pistol in the waist of his pants and went to her.

THREE

H left without waking the child or the mother. Outside, dawn haloed rows of triple-deckers. Power lines crossed the green-gray sky. A fingernail moon seemed hooked on a strand of clouds. Christine had left the Camry parked about eighteen inches and on an angle from a curb near the crosswalk. H got in. The cloth seats, plastic dash, vinyl steering wheel, and gearshift all felt refrigerated. Turning over, the engine wailed but started. He put the car into drive and left.

Thrumming over pavement, H watched his city. Water and silt darkened the snowbanks, which had thinned to reveal stretches of brick beneath. Runoff drained toward the bay. The streets, at this hour, were quiet. A guy wrapped up in a parka walked a shivering dog. A city bus, its insides lit and empty, hissed past. A siren chirped somewhere behind him. Two squirrels, swollen but mangy, pranced along a telephone wire. Winter had frozen and thawed so many times that the streets were crumbling and none of the animals seemed to know in which direction to fly. The weather on this planet had gone scurvy. H had skated on enough ponds in November, in March, to know the difference.

At the Irish market at the bottom of the hill, H pulled over and left the engine running and the hazards clicking and went inside. The shopkeeper, standing behind the Keno machine and before shelves of candy bars and cigarettes, seemed structural to the building, like a fifth wall or an upright floorboard. He wore sideburns that tracked his jawline, and he rang H up for a coffee without a word, charging the price of a small for a large. H paid, thanked the guy, returned to the car—which had warmed—switched on his phone and the radio, and began.

The first ride requested a pickup from an address near Brookline Village. On the way across town, the morning news fussed about elections, reported on these politics unhinged, of grown men lording over the debate with thumbs tapped against telephone screens, with sound bites raked from the fire of a screaming match on cable TV. There had been a budget proposal. A bill was taking shape. But the math tallied senators, not voters, approval ratings, not taxes paid. H felt a witness to some sort of plague. He'd refresh the news waiting for sanity to restore. Instead, every elected official squealed and squawked like a child holding his breath. H missed the dignity government had been afforded by his own ignorance. He wished it weren't so easy to know better. Frustrated, he switched off the radio and listened to tires rotating over pavement. The coffee rattled through him, and the car smelled of heat. He rubbed an eye, removed his toque, used the blinker to signal turns, and felt the road as though it'd been opened for him alone. The bruises on his face had temperature, geography. He thought of embers left burning in a fireplace overnight. A memory flashed of that bruiser descending, and H shivered.

From a brownstone near Coolidge Corner, across from the Publick House, came a man in a gray trench and fedora holding a briefcase by the handle. The man entered the car, and sitting unbelted with the satchel on his lap, watched out the window as H drove him to the airport. Sharing space, a ride, with this other body made H feel a part of something. Though the passenger didn't speak, he also didn't ask for the radio, and he didn't engage with his phone, either. Instead, they passed through the city in silence, through the Jewish neighborhood and by the shop windows along Beacon Street, the pubs and concert halls near Fenway, then under the city, under the bay, to the terminal at Logan. There, the man, with only his briefcase and no luggage, left for a flight.

A second fare, from a teenager with a backpack, led to the prep school south of the city. H recognized the campus. Growing up, H's team would sometimes practice at this rink, and now and then, he and his boys would throttle their varsity squad in a scrimmage. The passenger in the back seat wore a necktie and a parka, and during the trip, he fiddled with a tablet and kept headphones over his ears. They arrived, and he mumbled thanks and let himself out into the morning.

Soon, traffic thickened. H crisscrossed through the city, bringing a father and his two kids to a daycare in a gentrifying neighborhood in Southie. He took a commuter from the train at Back Bay to the biotech corridor in Cambridge and, from there, a professor-type to a campus on the north shore. He drove and watched these city people scurry through their mornings. All the women looked dressed for yoga. All the men were six foot six with shoulders wide and waists thin. They shared his city but seemed to be another species. Everything looked like

19

money: shoes, backpacks, watches, hats, haircuts, manicures, dog leashes, cell phone cases. Customers brushed off the seats before they sat down. They took calls, answered emails, and from the back of H's car, said, to him, little more than hello.

Then the roads turned lousy, but H—paid by the minute and the mile—didn't mind. He let other drivers in, let them turn left, braked for buses and at the crosswalks. He'd mounted his phone to the dashboard to display for passengers the route and the meter. The city provided just enough lanes to keep the pace slow, to keep anyone in a rush clutching the steering wheel with both fists. The fares added up. Hours passed.

By eleven, H had earned sixty-three dollars. He drove to a Holiday Inn near Mystic River, where through a corporate partnership, drivers could park and use the bathroom and fill up water bottles and take free coffee and buy breakfast from the buffet. Others had come too. In the lobby, drivers drew tepid eggs from a tray with a slotted spoon. They made toast and waffles, snatched and peeled runt-bananas, ate cups of children's yogurt. Some guys—and they were all guys—waited until eleven to make two meals of their money. H poured a coffee and sat in the dining room beneath a muted television. Steam lifted from his cup.

That morning, he'd made a sandwich by the light of the clock on the stove. Jo seemed able to sense his movement. She wailed whenever something happened without her. At night, when she finally went to sleep, and in the mornings, before she woke, they moved around like criminals in their own house. Snip which wire to deactivate the countdown? And which, then, made everything go boom?

H unwrapped his lunch and ate ham, American cheese, and

yellow mustard on white bread. Uncut, the sandwich sagged in the middle. The coffee tasted burned and weak but was warm and free. Some of the drivers made plates, sat together, and spoke in Spanish—Dominicans, H thought they were—about topics that made them whisper, then laugh, then shush one another. H closed his eyes and luxuriated in their modesty and stretched his feet out on the tile before him. He set an alarm on his phone to ring in twenty minutes.

After the assault, Sarah was taken to an urgent care in Hyannis. H had been old enough to sense tragedy, but too young to be interested in anything but the vending machines and the carpeted hallways and the television playing Disney movies. Every doctor, parent, and police officer kept asking him to leave her room. Had he stayed with his grandparents? He couldn't say. After that first night, they moved her to a hospital in Cambridge. Days passed. When Sarah came home, she was mute and pale. She said nothing for months. During that time, his parents argued with one another in whispers or spoke to H as if they had spoonfuls of sugar on their tongues. Anywhere H went, any move he made, his parents lunged as if diving before a shooter. He hadn't been able to chew without one or both asking if he was okay. They all but let the air out of his bicycle tires. He remembered being held from school for what felt like weeks, but for what must have actually been a day, or maybe two.

He'd been eleven when they brought her home. In those days, he'd felt as though he were in some sort of trouble, that their behavior was somehow his fault. He'd worried that they'd caught him doing something wrong and would confront him. He remembered cataloging his sins, wondering which had been discovered: H and his friends had been pushing around the

Nichols kid after school, he'd recently learned to swear and masturbate, his grades were maybe slipping, he'd taken to arguing with his teachers, he'd stolen french fries from the cafeteria, there was a girl he liked. At some point, someone must have said that Sarah was sick, though he didn't recall any one conversation or another. The facts were not made plain. No one sat him down on a bed and talked to him and said words like *rape* or *assault*. No one made him feel as though the silence, the tension, wasn't somehow his fault. By the time Sarah started talking again, the pills had taken hold. Then she began to lose weight.

When the pills ran out, she started breaking into his parents' liquor, then bringing her own into the house, hiding bottles behind curtains, in cereal boxes, in the toe of an old boot that no one wore, under the lawn mower during the winter and the snow blower during a heat wave. H would find them, and he remembered removing the caps, smelling the poison, flinching, but then replacing, say, a bottle of vodka behind the pipes of the basement sink, wondering what made this stuff so great. Wondering how come Sarah suddenly wanted only this. Curious, he'd steal a swig, but the taste made his face pucker, and the smell recalled fights and silence.

His parents must have explained somehow, and he understood, at some point, what it meant to be drunk, but never why it kept happening. And then she got herself into filthier things, more dangerous drugs. Then she would go missing for days at a time. Then she was snatching and pawning jewelry, raiding the house for valuables as though it were her own safety deposit box. She'd turn up in Houston or Florida. She'd need money for a flight home. His parents ran out of words altogether, and H found himself alone. He could only make sense of those years through his adult understanding of what had happened: that she'd been found by two friends that summer with Williams on top of her, with her shirt lifted up to her chin, with her jeans and underwear drawn down, in the basement of some rich kid's summer home, on a covered pool table, with a year's worth of dust blackening their clothing. One of the girls took the cell phone pictures that were used in court. Somebody called the police.

When and how did he come to know these details? Were any of them even true? Billy was the first man to mention Benjamin Williams to H in a decade. H remembered Williams only as a kid with a faint mustache sitting in a courtroom. He remembered a thin nose, a thin frame, dark hair, dark eyes and skin. Had they met? H doubted it. Had Billy even been there?

Sarah had been staying with Billy when the assault happened. Billy had been the one to let her go to the party. And he must have been, by geography if nothing else, the first to arrive at the hospital, the first to talk to the police, the face H's parents would have seen when they themselves arrived, frightened and furious and looking for a culprit. Where and when else had Billy been? H remembered a fistfight between his uncle and his father one Thanksgiving. There was a screaming match outside a rink in Taunton. Whatever else happened between his sister and his parents and his uncle, H had forgotten. Or else, they'd spoken their words behind closed doors and through drawn lips. Thanksgiving was the last time H remembered them all being together. Even though, for years, when his father wouldn't or his mother couldn't, Billy was the one to take him to hockey.

Who was the man who'd taken H to all those rinks, who'd watched every game, who would pour something into his coffee at the start of each period, who told H not to repeat any of this to his shrill mother, or to his washed-up father who had once been a riot, who'd once been a hero, but who'd altogether lost any sense of humor he had? Billy drove until H, tired of being asked by his parents what he and his uncle talked about, tired of being in the middle, found some other way to get around. Billy had been a friend—until he wasn't. Then he lifted from H's life. Years passed. Billy became the ruin he now was.

The alarm on H's phone buzzed. He'd been resting for twenty minutes, and he stood, freshened his coffee, and returned to the car. His phone, now activated, displayed the next fare: a pickup from one of those condo buildings near the casino. It wasn't yet noon.

He messaged Christine at a traffic light, asking after Jo.

At Mom's, she said, and included a picture of her mother seated on a carpeted floor before a smattering of toys. Legs folded beneath her, the woman held out a stuffed bear, and Jo sat red-faced and nose dripping, midscream. Something about capturing these moments—when Jo was at her worst, her most unhappy—pleased Christine. Without cynicism, she took and sent pictures of Jo in tears or upset or naked and crying, as if in defiance of the perfection that every other parent seemed desperate to curate and present. But then, Christine would leave the child with her mother to go swimming. Or she'd sit at the table and knit. Or she'd go and run some errand—to pick up shoelaces, to buy more paper towels—and H wondered if all her hiding and all these unhappy moments were related.

Pregnant, Christine couldn't walk past a bookstore without entering, finding the children's section, and sitting, cross-legged, to leaf through picture books and weep. She spent all of their money on things they'd never use: organic and BPA-free suckers, sippy cups, weighted blankets, and educational DVDs. They had three stuffed rabbits and a new onesie for each day of the month. Paint color samples—yellows and pinks—still shingled the walls of the nursery. Then Jo came, and Christine, suddenly, couldn't decide on anything.

The phone routed H to a pickup at Assembly Row—a half-constructed monstrosity of retail, luxury condos, and parking lots waiting to become one or the other—and he wondered if Jo had had the full term, the extra four weeks, would Christine have been able to prepare? Had the cost of the baby's early arrival been struck against the mother? Hard to imagine when Christine, in those days, looked weary but well and Jo arrived frighteningly weak: sunken eyes, red-faced, too tired to wail, arms like matchsticks, legs that didn't fill out the diaper. The daughter had been fragile, yet the mother had come apart.

Christine didn't say shit about how she felt. She didn't say shit about whatever went through her head. And H never asked. They had the kid. What more was there to say to one another?

H looked at his face in the mirror. His reddened eyes, the bruises blotting his cheeks, and the nick on his ear all transformed him into something unparental. Call child services. Round up the dog catcher. He was sure there were taxes to pay.

When H was a child of eleven years old, his sister went to a party at some Cape house, and she drank too much and took some pills and was raped by another kid named Benjamin Williams. Billy was supposed to be looking after her that summer. Billy had let her go to the party. The police came and told their mother and father, and then a decade seemed to pass: Sarah's doctors, illnesses, depression, the trouble with her pain pills and the drugs that followed. Then his father vanished into his work. Then cancer came for his mother, her chemo started, and she spent days and weeks in hospitals, sneaking cigarettes, and clinging to her anger until the day she died.

And then, as if the power came back on, as if all anyone needed was for dear old mom to croak, the healing started. Worse than all the trouble was everyone's healing. There were treatments, psychiatrists, support groups, and chaplains. Everybody grasped for and found something like daytime-talk-show faith, something that sounded like gospel but that came with a newsletter about the latest diet craze. His father retired to Key West. His sister's hair grew back, and her looks returned, and she fell in love with a man who'd recovered from his own busted-up background.

What should H feel now that everybody else but him and Billy was doing fine, now that his sister had built a career and was raising two darling children? Should he reconcile? How could anyone forget their mother, who'd died as furious as the cancer that had killed her, who'd gone down swinging at the air before her? Mom, the shadow-boxer, had departed spewing vitriol into every smiling face that came her way.

H pulled up in front of a department store and opened the glove compartment and waited for his passenger. The gun was there. He felt an urge to take and hold the weapon. Billy was confused. He'd mistaken H for somebody who didn't drive for a car service, who didn't have an infant and a girlfriend who was spinning off the planet. Benjamin Williams was the boogeyman, a bump in the night, as real as a cartoon character and as menacing too.

The passenger came and got into the back seat. H closed the glove box and started the ride.

That evening, a guy, midtwenties or so, summoned H to an office in the Seaport. He wore his hair cropped short and that same thousand-dollar parka that everyone seemed to own. When he came to the passenger side, the guy asked, with a knock, if he could sit up front. H waved him in.

Seated and buckled, the guy pointed at the photo of Jo that H kept clipped to the air conditioning vent.

"She's cute," he said. "Is she your daughter?"

H smiled. "How would this go if she weren't?"

"My old man always said, 'Do everything you want to do in life before you have a kid. Having a kid is a funeral.'"

H moved the car into gear and drove from the shoulder. "She's harmless."

"He said, 'Getting married is like putting your balls in a desk drawer and slamming it shut.'"

"I'm not married," H said.

"Of course, my dad has been married to my mom for forty years. She saved his life. He couldn't buy underwear without her. Are you going to propose to your girl?"

The streetlights, the headlights, and the rows of glass office buildings greened the edges of an inky sky. At rush hour or during the evenings on weekends, this stretch of the city, once only docks and fish markets, bristled with traffic, horns, people, and money, all moving. But now that the commuters had left for the night, the streets were empty and the gulls returned to pick at the scraps, squawking and lending this place something like geography, like setting. H believed he could feel the sea.

"She'd like that," H said, at last. "But she's not thinking things through."

"Mind if I ask what happened to your face?"

H touched his cheek. "What answer are you hoping for?"

"I'm not sure. Just—it looks like real life. I live in a snow globe." The guy pointed to the city beyond his window, the banks, and the café patios. "A bad day for me is a snippet of code I can't figure out how to write."

"I play hockey."

"For the Bruins?"

H laughed again. "Would I be driving on a Tuesday night? I play minors. A team you and nobody else ever heard of." H sized the kid up. There were shoulders beneath that jacket. "You play?"

"Once I did. Now I box," the guy said. "My coach is a former flyweight champion."

"Sounds serious."

"It isn't. I go to this boutique gym, the sort of place that promises to make you look better naked and offers eleven-dollar smoothies at the end of a workout. We don't actually fight. It costs too much money for them to let me get hit. What if it hurts? There's a yoga place right across the street. If I punch the bag too hard, they tell me to mind the upstairs neighbors. But sometimes you want a bit of red meat, you know?"

"Why pay so much if it's not what you want?"

"I don't," the guy said. "My company pays."

H whistled.

"My company pays for everything."

"Must be nice."

"It's not altruism," he said. "They've run all the numbers. They have a financial interest in making sure I don't come into the office brimming with adrenaline and looking to fuck non-stop. Everybody gets to comp an expensive hobby. They call it a perk, but it's more like a security policy."

"Seems like a deal to me."

"Look around, man. There aren't any deals left in this city. Every gesture is in service of the hive." He tapped the screen of H's phone. "Same as you," he said. "The company you drive for designs promotions to get you to take one more trip, to put in one more hour, to get you to work without a union or benefits or any of that New Deal stuff. They make it feel like it's your choice, but you're the customer, not the employee. They're selling to you. Trust me. I do this stuff for a living."

"I signed up online," H said. "I do everything through the phone. Nobody sells me anything."

"That's exactly right. They've designed it to be zero-touch so that you slide into the work. It's in the way the tool functions, the tech, the look of it. They know how you'll feel when you log on, when you see money added to your account, when you get a tip or a good rating."

H shook his head. "I'm in charge of my day."

"Come on," the guy said. "Those are their words coming from your mouth. It's not mind control, but it's something close. They've got doctors who understand the brain's pleasure centers. They've designed noises and colors and sounds to make you feel a certain way—the sequence isn't much different from a toy you'd buy for your baby. You're carrying a casino in your pocket, and all the odds are on the house."

"You're overthinking it," H said. "I do this a few days a week, when I'm not skating. This isn't a career."

"There's that word. Filthy, isn't it?"

"What you do seems interesting. We're all going to end up with some life's work. Might as well choose something important."

"What I do isn't interesting or important. I move information from one part of the computer to another. The second they've got an algorithm that writes algorithms, I'll be like you: driving for a living," he said. "No offense."

"Like I said, it's just a paycheck."

"Let me ask you, Is it enough? Can you pay rent?"

"I get a bit of money from hockey. Between the two, we get by."

"God, I wish I had the courage. I'd drive all day, listen to the radio, meet people. Accomplish exactly zero."

"I'm driving you home," H said. "I'm accomplishing that."

"But be free, right? Have your own conversations, or don't. Think your own thoughts, or don't. Go nowhere—literally drive in circles—and make a wage for your time."

"There's more to it than that," H said.

"There isn't. That's the whole point. Everything they tell me in my building is part of a story designed to get me to do one thing or another. But it's all breadcrumbs placed by somebody with a business plan."

"So quit, if it's so bad. The city could always use another driver."

"Pay's too good, man. I'm twenty-four. I've got time to be redeemed, or not. I can decide later."

"Maybe I'm the same way," H said. "Maybe I'm going for a master's degree. I might be next in line for your job when you leave. I'm twenty-four too, you know."

The guy looked him over. "You seem older."

"It's the miles."

"Hey." He pointed to a gray condominium building. "That's where I live. Listen, how do I win a fight? What's the trick to really fucking somebody up?"

"Are you in some kind of trouble?"

He shook his head. "Just in case. You know, everybody's blood's up in the bars these days. This city's got too few women for too many men. It's primal out there. What's the trick?"

H laughed. "The trick?"

The guy nodded.

"The trick is that nobody wins a fight, man. Nobody. It just hurts. Take it from me."

"Come on. There's got to be something you can give me."

"Protect the head."

"And the nuts?"

"Protect the head, protect the nuts, and whenever you can, the first chance you get, stay out of it."

Another car was pulled over in front of the building and the hazards came on.

"There's my dinner. I order a ride and food from the same app at the same time every day so both get home at once." He offered a hand. "Good talking to you."

"This is temporary," H said, shaking. "This is nothing to me but a few bucks in my pocket."

"Maybe I'll see you tomorrow. I ride pretty much the same two trips every day." He opened his car door. "There and back. I'd be glad to talk more. Keep fighting, brother," he said, pointing at H's face.

"Yeah, you too."

The guy closed the door and left.

Most mornings, as the car heated up, H opened the glove box, opened the bag, and took out the gun. What drew his hand to the weapon? H couldn't be sure. Start with: there it was, in the car, only a reach away. Start with: he'd never seen one up close, never outside of the movies, never held one, never fired anything. The windshield hadn't yet defrosted. His coffee was too hot to sip. Four thirty in the morning, and the streets were silent. His phone hadn't lit yet with the first ride of the day. H wanted to go for it. How about that? How about, H wanted to feel that metal against his skin.

He unfurled the bag. The heft of the pistol slid with a crumple to his palm. Laying there—taller than thumb to heel, longer than wrist to fingertip—the weapon felt significant. The weight measured something like three pucks. He tossed the paper to the passenger seat.

The handle curved and widened into an arc at an angle that seemed to draw itself into the flat of his hand, that seemed to command the fingers to wrap into place. A screw secured two crescents of wood, the surfaces of which were lacquered to a shine and cross-hatched with texture. He'd heard the expression before—describing, say, eyelets on boots, a belt buckle, the color of a luxury car—which was now given context: gunmetal. The barrel snuffed after two inches. There, to create a sight, metal ramped into a point in line with a notch at the handle. Pull on a lever, and the chamber gaped—a baby bird begging for food. H spun the empty cylinder, pushed the extractor, which resisted, which snapped forward when he withdrew pressure. He jerked his wrist to clap the weapon shut. He drew back the hammer, which clicked into place and slackened tension in the trigger. At his touch, the weapon lurched, trigger and hammer forward. The chamber advanced for the next round.

A hockey stick—straight, flat—needed an application of tape before it felt at ease in the hand. Ribs, notches, and knobs had to be added for grip. This pistol felt somehow athletic, instinctual. It extended him. He held the gun and understood that it was made to be held, that it had been designed to be cradled and used. Before Billy came, H hadn't thought about Benjamin Williams in years. Since Jo was born, he'd taken his licks on the ice, but he'd become a dove. He tiptoed into and out of every conversation. He never raised his voice. First came the baby's needs, then Christine's, then anybody else's, and only then, very last and least, what H wanted. Whatever might be done, or not, about Benjamin Williams sat at number one hundred on his list.

Each morning, his phone pinged from a ride being requested. H returned the pistol to its bag and the package to the glove compartment. His cell, in comparison, felt as smart and as thoughtful as a brick: square, dense, clumsy. Every proportion seemed wrong. Why so thin? Why so wide? Why all these edges? Why nothing for the fingers to feel for and press? The phone wanted his mind: look and touch, see and consume, and good luck finding your way free. The gun, though, seemed a part of him, as natural as a nose. Was it, with the pistol put away, loneliness he felt? That tingle like what sends an amputee scratching toward the end of the stub?

His phone would ping, and H would accept a fare and route toward pickup. His coffee, by then, would be tepid.

FOUR

H woke and went to take a leak and found, in the bathroom, his daughter, buckled into her car carrier and set on the floor of the tub. The shower curtain had been drawn aside. Light fell onto the child from through the frosted window. A stuffed butterfly hung from the faucet above her. Jo held a hand mirror. At the sight of her father, she gurgled and swung her arms. She was trying to clap.

H crouched. A film—gray and yellow—ringed the porcelain tub.

"Preening," he said to the girl. "And just what do our gospels say about vanity?" He touched her nose with the pad of his thumb. "It's a sin. Especially for the beauties among us."

She grasped for his finger, which he let her take, but then he stood and emptied his bladder. H washed, brushed his teeth, then came from the bathroom with the baby in one arm and the car seat in the other. Jo held the mirror to her chest. In the kitchen, among the hum of the monitor and the patter of talk radio, sat Christine, with needles clicking as she drew yarn from a ball on the table and set stitches into a scarf.

"Somebody was at the spas," H said. Jo's high chair was at the table, and as H lowered her into it, she braced her feet and pushed herself toward her mother.

"You groan when you pee," Christine said, tapping the monitor with a needle while leaving her eyes on her work.

"This girl has her mother's determination." H took Jo's ankles together and threaded her into her chair. Set, she slumped forward and squirmed to escape. He handed Jo a plastic book, the spine of which she inserted into her mouth.

"You came home late last night," Christine said.

"I thought you were sleeping."

"You were exhausted. I could hear it in your footsteps."

"You looked asleep."

"I wasn't."

"Ah," H said to the baby, "Mom was pretending."

"I was trying to sleep." Christine paused her knitting to look at him. She'd pulled her hair into a bun atop her head, and her face, untreated, had the color of fallen snow.

"You say it like I stole from you. Do I have it all wrong? It's happened before." He turned to the child, made a face. "What do you think? Out of bounds? Strike the comment from the record. Why can't your old man ever stick to the facts?" H took a carton of Cheerios from the cupboard and toppled a measure onto the tray before Jo. She looked up at him, smiled, clasped a piece of cereal, and thrust it into her mouth with the top half of her fist.

"And then what?" he asked.

"'Then what,' what?"

"Did you see me fall asleep?"

"You were mumbling," she said. "Talking. Then you started to snore."

"When did you sleep?"

"Is it time again for my physical?" She offered a wrist. "Here, doc, feel my pulse."

"Did you sleep at all, Christine? Three hours? One?"

"Baby the baby, please, if you're looking for someone to mother. She could use a good influence in her life."

Jo slapped a palm on her tray and squealed. Two against one.

H poured himself a bowl of cereal, took milk from the fridge and added some. Christine had measured and left coffee grounds and water in the pot, and he pushed the button to brew. "And Joanna, here, needed some time to herself this morning? Is that it?"

"She hates the sound the needles make," Christine said.

H looked at the child, who with eyes like globes, with silvery, wet gums, smiled as she watched Christine knit.

"What sort of mother would I be if I provoked her?" Christine shook her head. "I moved her into the bathroom, where she could be comfortable."

"Not the bedroom."

"Right."

"So you could knit," H said.

"So you could sleep," Christine said. "I dote on you both equally, in case you mean to make a competition of it."

"I see." H leaned against the counter and ate some cereal. "The knitting is urgent."

She nodded.

"More urgent than the needs of our little one here?"

"Don't make math of it, H. Don't turn it into a rap sheet.

I committed to a hundred scarves by Christmas. That's what I signed up to do." Christine paused her knitting and turned her eyes on him so that the browns of her irises seemed to deliver an accusation. "And anyway, don't be so close-minded," she said.

"I didn't know that I knew how."

"I can mother and knit and be a girlfriend all at once. Would you have me give up on myself altogether? Didn't you fall in love with that girl we call Christine?"

He finished the last of the cereal, tipped the bowl to his mouth and drank the leftover milk, then wiped his lips with a wrist. "We can have it both ways, is that it? All three ways?"

"I'm a modern woman, H. I'm a twenty-first-century woman. Have you forgotten what it means to compromise?"

"You ought to run for mayor."

She nodded once, chin to chest, as though she were depositing the idea from her head to her heart, for keeping. "Jo shouldn't get one hundred percent of my attention."

"That would be too much."

"But what she does get is just enough"—Christine reached out, still holding the needle, rotated her wrist, and with the back of her hand, touched the girl's cheek; Jo snatched for her mother—"so that she knows that I love her and that I care about the greater world."

"And the necks of those in the greater world."

"And the cold necks of those poor women and men who are living hard in that greater world."

"And the swimming too, don't forget that."

"Would that we could solve the world's problems with scarves alone, H."

"We need to swim laps too."

"We need to raise money. To raise money, we need to build awareness. To build awareness, we swim. It's all part of the same movement."

"The movement," he said. "How could I forget the movement?"

"I'm setting an example, H. She watches me. What would I be teaching her if I let our poorest freeze and go hungry?"

"What do you think, darling?" H stood and swept Jo from her seat, lifting her high above his head. "Do I have it all wrong? Do we take her at her word?"

The coffee pot churned. H brought their daughter to the couch and onto his lap, offering her four fingers—two per side—which she took. She pulled herself to her feet and stood on his thighs—a circus act. The Amazing Jo! Hold your breath and watch! Christine set her work aside, stood, and went to the blender. From the refrigerator, she withdrew the ingredients for her smoothie: kale, berries, carrots, some sort of powder, almond milk, flax.

"Is your mother setting an example, Jo? Is that what we're meant to see?" He mimed taking a bite of her thigh and blew air against the child's skin. Tickled, she giggled. "Or, perhaps, might there be some other motive? What do they call it in the movies, honey?"

"Ulterior."

"Ulterior," H said to the baby. "That's a word you'll learn."

Christine poured coffee and brought it to him, black. "She was perfectly happy in the tub," she said, handing him the mug. "I was listening. She had her butterfly and her mirror. Children need time to themselves. Us mothers can sense this. Female in-tuitions, H. Have you seen how they whip and snap?"

"Are you going to add some sugar to that," H said, looking at the garden on the counter.

"Thank you for your concern, H. It tells me that you're a good father. I chose a good one. On an evolutionary level, I'm pleased. But remember, I know just when our daughter needs her mother, and just exactly when she needs some time to herself."

"It smells like a forest in here. Remind me again, What's in a flax seed?"

"Flax seed," Christine said, pushing the button to activate the blender.

And as if on cue, outside, the engine of a pile driver rumbled into gear. A vehicle, reversing, began to beep. H looked at the clock: 11:44 a.m. The crew outside had finished lunch. H brought the baby to the window, and she stood on the back of the couch and pressed her hands to the glass. Outside, men had laid the foundation for a new condo building. A school bus idled at a stoplight. Men and women moved down the sidewalks with their shoulders shrugged up around their necks, with their hands in their pockets. The sky threatened rain. He watched a woman balancing a duffel on her head enter the laundromat across the street. The traffic light changed and somebody leaned into a car horn. A jet passed overhead. Beside him, a length of aluminum siding riled in the wind and whapped against the house.

Jo sneezed, and H realized how cold it felt in the apartment. Wasn't it April? The planet seemed in cosmic distress. They were aliens on their own rock. If they didn't spin right off this orbit, he'd be the first to admit his surprise. Jo turned to watch the men below. Get one last look, H thought. One day, you'll tell all your pals about this twenty-first-century American living. Won't it seem quaint. Won't you shake your head and laugh at our once-good fortunes. You'll be old, then, he thought, and we'll have ruined everything, but you'll remember apartment buildings and combustion engines and walk-in closets for the masses, for the people—unalienable, as if ratified in the constitution. Jo sneezed again.

The blender quieted, and Christine poured some of the sludge into a glass. H felt the wood floor against the palms of his feet. They'd had this conversation before, hadn't they? What was his part?

"Add some sugar to that," he said. "Or cinnamon. There can't possibly be any calories in cinnamon. Add some honey, honey. I never saw an overweight bee."

"Bees make the honey," Christine said. "They don't eat it."

"Peanut butter, then."

"H, there's points in that. Do you want to know how it works, or do you just want to pester me?"

"Number two," he said, and then he shivered. The floorboards felt cold. The air felt damp. "Where does all the heat go?" H said. "I know we paid for an appearance. Heat? I bought a ticket. I demand a show." He smooched the baby's belly, then took her hat from the couch cushion and pulled it over her ears. She pawed at the window.

"She'll fall if you don't hold her up."

"She's balancing. Watch how she applies herself." H tapped on the window. "See, kid, that's called progress. Can you say *gentrification*?"

She patted the glass.

"Say *doggie daycare*? No? *Hipster coffee*? *Mommy and Daddy relocate to Tulsa*?"

Jo, looking at her own reflection, smiled.

"She came to watch you sleep this morning."

Condensation had collected and frozen along the aluminum frame of the window, which was cold to the touch.

"She opens the bedroom door," Christine said. "I don't know how she does it."

H knocked on the glass. "This whole structure is shot. Jesus, the rent we pay. I read online what they plan to list those condos for. Just try and guess. Sit first, because you may lose your balance when I tell you."

"She crawled up to the bed, but I think she could see that you were sleeping. I think she was trying not to disturb you."

H could feel a draft, which seemed to be coming from behind him, from the kitchen to the window and out. He held a hand over the radiator. "Do you think the heat just comes up and goes straight out those windows? Straight up and out?" He took Jo under her arms and lifted her up above his head, tossing her once, then swinging her down to the couch. She squealed with delight. "What do you think, honey?" he said, into her belly.

"H," Christine said.

He swooped Jo from the cushion, up across the room, making the sound of an engine, then over to the thermostat. "Sixty-seven!"

"H, you'll rile her up."

He put his nose to the baby's belly and made a show of sniffing. "Smell that, darling."

"H, please."

"Your mother's burning through all that cash we'll never have." He motored the kid to the floor and simulated the sound of a crash. "It's an inferno. The planet burns." H turned from

Jo to adjust the heat down. "If it's going to be cold, we might as well not pay for it."

"Goddamn it, H," Christine said.

H turned to ask what, but then the baby was screaming.

Christine set her drink aside and came and took Jo to her chest. "Please," Christine was saying, "No, no, honey. He doesn't know. It's all right, hmm? It's all right, baby."

Jo's face had transformed, had gone red. She'd been smiling ten seconds ago, but now she wailed. And H wondered, had he set her down hard, had something hurt her? How had he so offended? Her mouth bobbled and her lips shimmered and she cried out with something like agony. Christine, patting the child's back, bobbing in place, began to smile, then giggle. And then, she was hysterical, laughing, gasping, shushing herself, and whispering, "Fuck, fuck, fuck." H raised a hand to reach for them—one or both—but stopped. Christine kept swearing. Her hand on Jo's back made the girl sound hollow, like a drum, like a palm thwapped against stretched flesh. The baby wailed, and Christine rocked and hummed a melody that the child ignored, that Jo seemed to loathe, that she seemed to indicate, with her cries, was beneath her. Couldn't they see that she was human and furious? Didn't they know that a song offered nothing to ease her pain?

Mother and child watched the room before them, and their cheeks were slick with tears.

Was there enough air in here for them three? Why wouldn't Christine look at him? How come any nudge sent her crumbling apart?

He had to get to the rink, H thought, and then he told them so. "I should get to practice," he said, over the girl's cries.

Then he told Christine about work too, about how he ought to drive a shift after he skated. "To make some extra cash," he said.

"I hate this," Christine told him back.

"I could probably make a hundred," he said, "maybe a hundred and fifty."

"I hate it so much."

"It would be a few hours," H said. "I could be home at seven. I could be home by seven or eight."

"Go away," she said.

"That's right." H nodded. "I should get to practice, to work."

To the baby, she said, "Shush, shush, shush." Christine hiccuped. Her hair, he saw, was tangled. Stains pocked her T-shirt: food, vomit, snot, tears. Where had all that weight come from in her cheeks, below the sockets of her eyes? When had her skin gone so gray? Veins twisted up both wrists and arms and appeared invasive, as if squeezing something from her. She held her daughter, and said, "Shh. Fuck. Shush, shush."

Jo quieted. H could hear air moving into and from her chest. He could hear a breathing that convulsed her. The baby shuddered, and H nodded. That was right. His keys, he felt, were still in his pocket from the night before. His gear was at the rink. The pistol was in the car. Or was it in his hand? Could he feel it there, like metal and fire against skin that, moments before, had held his daughter? Suddenly, the gun was all he could think about. He should leave that kitchen. He ought to go.

H told her, okay, he needed to leave, and Christine, looking down, looking off, nodded yes.

FIVE

During a drill, Coach gave H a whack on the shoulder with his clipboard. "Come see me later," he said, and then he skated off and blew his whistle to send the boys racing up the ice.

H watched Coach glide away on legs as stiff as pegs. Change the setting on the thermostat, and the old man might topple, belly-first. Who stacked the deck for men like these? Who gave Coach the pen and the list? Muscle that H had shaped over a decade of conditioning slackened at a word whispered, at a look steered just north of eye contact. The whistle chirped again, and H went chasing after the others, wheeling to make up the ground.

Coach ran them ragged: up, back, stand on the line, go, stop, then go again. They waited for their orders, shoulder to shoulder, like puppies at mealtime. In the cold, their breath clouded before them, and when Coach said to, they went. H's pulse thundered. The pipes to his lungs didn't seem wide enough. He felt his body tiring, betraying him. When had he last slept through the night? When was the last minute he had to himself? The others seemed to float, and he felt like an old man, a father, as though he'd been looking for a bathroom, but he'd somehow walked onto the stage. When the buzzer sounded, ending practice, H took a knee until his vision righted. Then he followed the others to the lockers, where he showered and dressed. Twenty minutes later, he found Coach seated in the bleachers watching a team of youngsters—six, seven years old—topple through cones and swarm after loose pucks.

Coach sat—folded sports section in hand, driver's cap low on his brow—and wrestled with a wad of gum that bulked in the pocket of his cheek. The lump smelled of foregone cigarettes. His mustache tottered, and his lips smacked, making a sound like a straw sucking at the dregs of a milkshake. His belly splayed across his lap.

H took a seat one row down. For a while, they watched the ice. One of the kids—young, H thought, Jo plus a few years—was pushing a chair, using its four legs to keep up on his two. H remembered himself at that age: skating like drawing breath. You'd have thought he'd been born onto the ice. You'd have felt like a witness: Praise be the Lord! This boy, here, walks on frozen water. Play the lottery! Phone the local news!

"This kid." Coach pointed. "Number twelve, here—watch him go."

"He's a big pup," H said.

"Size isn't it. See him set his edges?"

H looked.

"See his eyes? He's watching the far net. He's sniffed it out. Want to know what's going on in his head?" Coach made a sound like static on a TV. "His feet have got a mind of their own. They're running the show."

H could see that the boy could skate, that he didn't bumble along with the others. "He might be older than the rest."

Coach snorted.

"He's bigger," H said again.

"It's his feet," Coach said. "See? Anyway, you can't say a thing for sure about size when they're at this age. Who knows which one sprouts or not? For that, you've got to have a look at the mother."

"The father?"

"The mother. The mother's the lower bound: boy'll be at least that big. Size isn't it, though. You know that."

"Maybe."

"Size isn't what anyone recruits for—at least not where it matters."

"I heard about kids drafted out of high school just for being six six, six seven."

"Urban legend," Coach said.

"A guy I knew heard from a guy he skated with."

"That's fantasy, son. It's a story they tell to keep you small guys hungry. Yeah, okay, so even if the big fellow gets drawn, he still has to know how to move. If that isn't learned by age five, it won't ever be. You know that. Getting drawn and going nowhere is worse than never getting drawn."

"Is that right?"

"At least you got ice here. At least you've gotten action. How'd it feel to pop all those goals your rookie year? What'd you net, seventeen? Eighteen?"

"Eighteen."

"Felt like magic, didn't it? Nobody gets that memory but you. This is elite level. Kids from every frozen field in Canada and from every union town in Minnesota work their whole lives for this. Did you forget that?"

H thought about that first season when he was nineteen. He'd seen lights in the stands and had believed in where the game might take him. Then, it'd felt like the beginning of something. Now, it seemed the mark against which every other accomplishment was measured. He shook his head.

"How's your face?"

H put the back of his fingers to his cheekbone. "It's nothing."

"It's gone white."

"That's just healing."

"It's a good shiner. Lucky for you he didn't catch your nose, your teeth."

"Half aren't mine already anyway."

"Just the same. Who's got money for a dentist?"

H shrugged.

"The nose breaks easier every time. A concussion's like that too."

H shrugged again. "Everybody says my face is too pretty."

Coach smiled. "The sound it makes," he said. "The nose." He shook his head. "Like a melon dropped from a window. It's pure violence. Anyway, I'm thinking about sitting you, son."

H nodded. Overhead, four large air conditioners hummed. H had never been cold in a rink before, but he drew his jacket closed. The thing about pulling one over is that it can be a relief to get caught. Finally, finally, they were all talking about the same thing, speaking the same English. For a minute or two, H watched his boot laces.

"I like to look at these kids," Coach said, pointing, "because I like the way they play: with singularity. Know what I mean?"

H didn't. Was *singularity* the word? He shook his head.

"They get lost. They've got tunnel vision only. Sometimes a kid'll get so turned around he takes the puck in the wrong direction, gets all the way up to his own net and shoots before he realizes he's gone backward. You ever seen something like that?"

The kids were running a skating drill around each of the circles, forward in one direction, then stopping to pivot and move in the other. One in a blue helmet took a tumble at center ice, and an assistant skated over, scooped him up, and righted the boy.

"Sure," H said. "When I was little, maybe."

"How about that for a way to play?"

"Lost?"

"Involved. Excited. Dying to be a part of it. So wrapped up in the game you don't know which way's up. If you can find a kid like that, you can teach him everything he needs to know."

H thought of his early days: barefoot and dressing on rubber mats, his old man would lace up his skates, Billy watched from the stands, pancake breakfasts afterward, crisscrossing the state, going from one rink to the next. "I don't remember being on the ice at that age," he said. "I *was*, of course."

"There you go. You know those shifts where you get off the ice and you realize you can't think of a thing that happened out there? You take the bench, and one of the guys says, 'How about that pass,' or 'Good look,' and you've got no idea what he's talking about. You understand what I'm saying?"

H nodded.

"That's the stuff, kid. That's it. You're involved. You're reacting. You and the others are gears in the machine, turning together like you've got no mind at all. That's what I need from you. That's why we practice. Right now, all you are is up your own ass. You're overthinking it."

H laughed. "It's been a while since anyone's brought that charge."

"You're overintellectualizing the game, and you're just not smart enough for that to be anything but an anchor."

Coach added another piece of gum to the pile and kept on smacking. For a while, they sat and watched the kids skate. Three men—fathers—had gathered at the far corner of the rink. Each had rested a paper coffee cup on the outside ledge of the boards. The plexiglass, scratched and worn, obscured the men's faces, but H felt as though he knew them. Easy to imagine that their children, only a few years ahead of Jo, had worn them into anonymity, had turned them into the forms H now saw. How do you solve confusion? Exhaust it. Deprive it of sleep and free time. Make strangers of your own thoughts. There you go, H figured, watching those men. There's one way forward.

And then, in a few years, those three would look less like H and more like Uncle Billy: bellies, bald spots, bad breath, clothes that didn't fit right. They'd have wives that couldn't stand them. They'd have kids who didn't appreciate all the basic, being-alive shit that they did every day: making food, straightening up, earning a paycheck. And then? Then, they'd be grateful for the fifteen, twenty minutes they got to themselves when they took a shit. A hot shower could be a reprieve.

Or, like Billy, they'd look at the balance sheet. They'd start counting up all the bad breaks. They'd wish that they would have acted sooner. Not everyone had a nephew.

H ran his hands through his wet hair, which smelled sweetly of soap.

"I don't need you to take every possible beating," Coach said. "It fires the boys up, sure, but it's neutral. It's net-nothing. It doesn't help. This is the last time I'm asking."

"Some people say it's part of the game."

"This isn't history class."

"Maybe it's part of my game."

"You're, what, five eleven? You clomp around out there like you're King Kong. Here's the bottom line: if I wanted it to be part of your game, I'd tap you on the shoulder, and I'd say, 'H, go on out there and put that face of yours into harm's way.'"

"It gets the guys going. Reilly's game-winner—"

"Reilly's game-winner came from Michelson's backcheck, to Darius's breakout, and then to a hell of a snapshot. Your fight had been declared over four minutes earlier."

"Maybe my fight caused Michelson's backcheck."

"Maybe the dawn of mankind caused your fight, is that it? Maybe it was the Magna Carta. Manifest Destiny. Let me resay it in plainer English: fight again, and you're benched . . . Don't you want to ask me why?"

H dipped his head. "It's my game, Coach."

Coach blew a bubble, which popped. "But it's not your planet, is it? Everybody's dying, but nobody's christened you a thing. I need a third-line winger with enough speed on the outside to wreak havoc while I rest the Michelson line. I need a chip-and-chase attack. I need you dogged at all times. Thirty, thirty-five seconds of adrenaline, then come back to me. You are my boomerang. You're a puppy on a leash. If all this sounds like a grind, that's because it's meant to."

"That's that, then?" H said.

Coach took a napkin from his pocket and spat into it a wad

of gum the size of a golf ball. He took a drink from a canteen that had been resting on the bleachers beside him, then sighed.

"Kid, whatever kind of special you had at one time, you don't anymore. Don't take it personal. You're not the first guy on the planet to have a baby. I had kids once too, H. They're little vampires. They'll take every last inch you can give and still thirst for more. I don't blame you for slowing a step, but you can't seem to skate past another guy without thinking he owes you blood. And you're doing it, I think, because scoring goals and backchecking and coming to the bench fast and getting to open space is hard work. Taking and handing out fists is easy. It's lazy.

"H, I've got bigger guys for fighting. I've got younger guys to score goals. I don't need lazy. I need you to listen."

"Shut up, put my head down, and do as I'm told—is that it?"

"I hate to be the bearer of bad news, but welcome to planet Earth. You've got fifty more years. It won't seem so, but they pass in thirty-, thirty-five-second shifts, one after the next. Each is going to feel like a grind.

"I'm not saying that I can't use you in the role I can use you in. And nobody's saying you can't teach an old dog. Keep showing up. I've seen older guys rebound from worse, and I've seen better guys never come so far. You know, hit the gym. See if you can't get a stride faster. Maybe you start producing again and everything changes."

H nodded and folded his hands over his lap and felt through the fabric of his jacket the butt of the pistol. He'd forgotten that he had it in the inner pocket. The weapon, unloaded but heavy against his palm, calmed him.

"I need you to want it, son. I'll need you to want it enough to listen to me. That's how I'll know. That'll be the first thing I look for."

H nodded, though he wasn't sure he understood.

"You know, the sad thing about kids your age is that you've got no idea how fast it all goes. Chin up, son. This isn't an ending," Coach said. "And anyway, nothing personal."

"Sure, Coach." As if he had feelings left to trample. Try drawing water from dust. "Anything else?"

"Things change. I get it. A kid'll make you see the world another way, and that can be a blessing." Coach leaned back against the bleachers. "If things change for you, if you decide you've got other priorities, you let me know. No hard feelings."

"No hard feelings," H said, and then he stood.

Below, the kids had gathered at center ice, and some had taken two knees instead of one, and some sat or sprawled out on their backs. Their coach was trying to tell them something by drawing on a dry-erase board, but all those kids wanted, H could see, was to get moving again, was to turn their eyes back toward some point forward and go galloping, one stride after another.

On a Tuesday evening, H dropped his gear to the floor of the locker room and sat in his cubby, which boxed him in on three sides to about the width and depth of his shoulders. The guys wore headphones or chattered with one another: plays they'd missed, girls they'd had this week, or some of the greatest hits, which guys on the Bruins deserved their bench spot and which didn't. H sat and listened. Velcro peeled apart. Tape being unwound creaked like floorboards underfoot. Joints cracked inside rotating ankles, arched backs, clasped and outstretched hands and arms. The weather had gone cold and had chapped and pinkened H's hands, and when he tied his skates, wrapping the laces around his fingers to get leverage, the skin between his knuckles split, and he began to bleed. His leg, he noticed, was twitching. The nerves fired inside his chest. Was that what it meant to love your work? For it to feel at once familiar and always brand new? H didn't know.

When he dressed, he moved the pistol from his jacket pocket to the toe of his boot. None of the guys noticed because none looked at much else besides his own self. H wrapped his shin pads in tape. He snapped his helmet, tucked the sleeves of his jersey into the forearms of his elbow pads, and buckled his pants. Placing one knee down, one boot out, he stretched his hamstrings, one and then the next, and then his groin. They stood and queued. H followed the others, skate blades thwacking against rubber mats, out onto the ice. White and yellow light came from the ceiling, reflected off the ice and glass, and seeming everywhere at once, rendered them shadowless.

The boys from Rochester took the opposite side, and H, looking over, felt his fingers stir.

SIX

Christine had called and said she'd forgotten her gym bag. She asked him to collect it from the closet and bring it to her at the Y, which he did. When he got there, though, H felt the air— damp and heavy—and saw the chipped tile floors and the plastic ceiling, and he wished he hadn't come. The gym was empty. The desk sat unmanned. The baby, in her stroller, made two fists and fussed. A window in the lobby revealed the pool area, and H saw Christine sitting on bleachers by the shallow end, towel wrapped around her waist, rubber cap pulled over her head, goggles resting on her brow. In spandex, she looked like a doll stripped of clothing. She propped her chin on the heel of her palm. He could count the knobs on her spine.

H unzipped the bag and found not gear, but clothes, toi- letries, a couple of paperback novels. She was leaving.

He looked to Jo who smiled as though she'd known all along.

"Whose side are you on," he said to the baby, who only grinned back.

Because he couldn't think of anything else to do, H went

to Christine. His eye, which had been cut during a fight in the Rochester game, felt the sting of chlorine. He winced. The bruise would heal. Whatever word Coach had used after the last brawl—cut, suspended—meant that his career was over. He'd have time to repair.

Christine took a breath that lifted her shoulders and straightened her posture. She braced herself with palms against the bleachers, and H thought that maybe he should take those hands into his own. Instead, he set the duffel on the tile, lifted the baby from the carrier, and sat at a distance. The metal felt cold through his jeans.

For a while, they said nothing. Bluer water, a better view, and they might have been on vacation. Here, though, dampness—on towels, chairs, ceilings, and walls—spoiled any illusion. Christine wouldn't look at him.

"This is where you go," he said.

She shrugged. Her shoulders were still wet. She'd swum before calling him. She'd swum on it.

"It's quiet," she said. "I can think here."

"For me, that's the car," he said. "When it's empty or when the passenger's looking at his phone."

"I couldn't even tell you what I'm trying to work out. It's just—when else do I get to hear my own thoughts?"

"They've become strangers." H smiled and touched Jo's belly. "This one's made us strange."

She turned to him. "Your eye, H. It looks worse."

"It's healing."

"It looks terrible. It looks like carnage."

"It's only ruptured blood vessels. Doc said all my infrastructure's still intact."

"How am I supposed to listen when you say 'don't worry'? You're going to frighten the baby."

"It's yesterday's news, Christine. Coach doesn't want to carry me anymore, and no other team needs a body this age. You don't have to worry. The last fight was the last fight."

"That could be a blessing," she said.

"How much longer could I nurse the fantasy anyway? I was beginning to feel like a—an alchemist, trying to spin something from dust."

"It could be a beginning. You could finish school or find something else. You could do whatever you want."

"Good riddance, is that it? The smell of the game has been on my palms since preschool. A week out, and I can already taste the air again."

"You'll heal," she said. "You'll sleep. That's something."

"Don't worry so much about trying to make a sale. There is no option B. And anyway, I'm already on the mend. Watch me multitask." He turned Jo so they were facing one another. "She never seemed to notice the damage."

"She did. We both did. We hate to see you in pain."

"Is that why you never came to watch?"

"I came."

"Only my bum uncle to witness the one thing I'll ever do with my life."

"I did come." Christine turned to him. "Lots of times."

"Until."

She turned away. "Everything aches, H. My joints, my back. I wake up, and my teeth hurt. My palms have cuts in them from my fingernails."

"We're all a bit dinged up, is that it?" He looked at the baby. "Is that it, darling?"

Jo ignored them and instead seemed taken with the pool. Light lapped along the surface, and she reached for the movement with both arms. She looked to her father, but he felt no urge, no instinct, to engage with her. The baby, seeming to sense the mood, stilled.

"It's not as though I ever came here before."

"To watch me swim?"

"I'm proud of this."

She laughed. "You'd be bored almost immediately. *I'm* bored almost immediately."

"You're raising money for a good cause. That's good. I admire you for it."

She shook her head. "It's wrong to think this is altruism. What I'm doing here—running, hiding—is selfish. I do it for myself."

"You could have taken up cigarettes or gambling or, I don't know, fucking other people. What you're doing here matters."

"It's a hobby," she said. "It's nothing like what you did. How many people, H, get to where you got? A few thousand, maybe, in the world? I'm proud of that. I really am."

H laughed.

"What's funny?" she said.

"Where was all this before you'd made up your mind to leave?"

He put his boots out before him and leaned back against the bleachers and watched the scaffolding above him. He heard a door open and swing shut, and he turned to watch a man, old and round and tan on the chest and belly, come from the locker room and lower himself into the pool by the ladder. The baby cawed. She was becoming restless.

"So, you know," Christine said finally.

"Only just now. Only when I saw you dressed for the pool."

"That's why you waited by the door."

He shrugged. "How did you think I'd react?"

"It's just—" she said. "Now that you're not skating anymore. Now that you don't need to be at practice every day or traveling every week—it's just possible."

"Win-win, is that the idea? Thank goodness that pesky career of mine has finally ended."

She took her face into her hands and spoke through her fingers. "You could come with me," she said. "You both could."

"To your mother's?"

"There's plenty of room."

"Would that even help?" H said. "Would that even give you what you need?"

"Yes," she said. "Of course. How do I explain? Having my mother there—it would make everything different. I'm sure of it."

"You'd cage us two animals together?" He smiled. "I'm not sure we'd both survive."

"She'll mellow. The baby mellows her. All of those parental instincts get turned onto Jo."

H agreed, though what was the point. He'd taken on a slouch.

"You could ask me to stay," she said.

He nodded. That was true. The man in the pool paddled sidestroke. H listened to the whirl of water pulled, displaced, then settling back into stillness.

"Will you come back?"

"Yes," she said. "Of course."

"When?"

"You could ask me to stay," she said again.

H thought it over. He thought about the baby and the mother, alone together, each wearing the other ragged. He thought about the money he would make driving, one trip at a time, hour after hour. It wouldn't ever add up. He thought about picking a kindergarten, clipping coupons, buying secondhand clothing, dropping the girl off at daycare, scrambling for rent, scrambling for groceries, forgetting one another—forgetting to talk, forgetting to ask—growing apart, becoming spiteful. Christine staying would trigger a long line of misadventure that started here and ended there and that pained them—his only family—at each step along the way. Asking her to stay wouldn't be selfish, it would be ruinous.

Outside, in the glove box of the car, H had Billy's pistol. Somewhere, across town, lived the man who'd started all this. Did that man sleep, his conscience clean, while they all suffered? Could H ask her to stay? Of course he knew the words.

He stood and retrieved the bag for her. "Call us," he said. "Take whatever time you need and call us. We'll miss you, but we understand."

"There's formula on the shelf," she said. "I bought a tin today. You'll need to get more on Wednesday. On Tuesday you should get more."

"All right."

"The purple kind, H. It has to be the purple kind. The other stuff upsets her stomach."

"That's fine."

"Go to Market Basket. The prices are better," she said. "Tuesday. Don't forget."

"Yes," H said. "Tuesday."

"The extra diapers are in the closet under the stairs in the cardboard box. I didn't have a chance to put them away."

"That's fine. Thank you."

"And don't bother, H, with the big stroller. It's too big," she said. "Use the umbrella stroller." She wiped her cheek. "That's easier, and she likes it just the same."

"And naps?" H said, though he knew the answer.

She was nodding. "Twice a day: in the morning at eleven and then one in the afternoon. She gets so wired before bed, H. She gets so much energy. Don't rile her up. Read her something. Give her a bath. She'll tire."

"Yes," he said, "I know she will."

"She'll fight you, but she'll tire."

"I understand."

"I'm sorry," Christine said.

"I know." And to the baby H said, "All right." He took their daughter and left.

SEVEN

On the ice, the boys had taken possession low and were working up a cycle, and H, watching from the bleachers, thought they looked like they could move. He was wondering how he'd ever made this squad to begin with. Then Billy came out of the tunnel and up the steps and asked if he could sit.

"I'm not the usher," H said, looking at the bench next to him.

"I was across the way." Billy pointed. "I didn't see you on the ice, so I looked up. Nice necktie."

"A healthy scratch isn't the same as being cut. Coach wants me to represent the team."

"Paisley." Billy put his hands on his hips. From taking the ten or so steps, his breathing sounded damp and heavy. "Smart choice."

"These seats don't have numbers," H said. "If one looks open, it is."

Billy sitting was like a jumbo jet landing: he lined up, turned, readied, tested his knees, tested his ankles, then, thirty seconds later, he'd found a way to lower himself, with a bump, into place.

The boys were playing loose, chasing pucks and tossing bodies around like wrecking balls, but Billy, seated, wanted only to look at Jo. She was a sight, wrapped up in her snowsuit and wearing her beanie. Think H was made of stone? Blood, after all, pumped through his veins. Still, H watched his uncle watch his daughter and thought that the guy could spoil a winning lottery ticket.

"You want to stop looking at my kid like that and maybe pay attention to the game?"

Billy puckered his lips and made kisses, and the baby drew on her sucker.

"My niece," Billy said.

"Sarah's your niece. Jo's barely related to you. Jo's a baby sitting nearby. A police officer finds you two together, and you'd have explaining to do."

"My lineage."

"In fact, we're all praying she has exactly none of your DNA. The math works in our favor, but just in case, we've started a collection. Put some money in the fireman's boot."

"She has my eyes," Billy said, then he batted them for the baby like a starlet might.

"Watch the game, huh? You're upsetting the children."

"My eyes and my sense of humor."

"She eats like you. I'll say that. There's not a thread of clothing I've spent money on that she can't ruin just by having a meal."

"I should have had a kid," Billy said. "I should have had dozens."

"She takes shits that remind me of you. She messes herself, and I think, Oh, Uncle Billy."

"A brood. Oh, boy, more than I could have counted. So many that I'd mix them all up. Look how good she is. A regular angel. She doesn't even stir in all this noise."

H shrugged. Wasn't as though the stands were brimming. Wasn't as though they sold out crowds. He looked at the fans: fathers with small children eating popcorn from greasy paper bags, college kids sucking on malt liquor. From the stands, the production seemed small time. Still, the boys could move. They made a racket, streaking around the ice, and Jo listened and stayed quiet. From where had she learned these manners?

"She's only ever fully awake at three in the morning," H said. "At six in the afternoon, she'll sleep through the Four Horsemen. Come three, though, all she wants to do is tell you how horrible the world is."

"She looks like you too, H. One,"—Billy pointed to his chest—"two, three peas in a canoe."

"Could you watch the game, please?"

Billy cooed. "Poor thing. A sweetheart for a mother, and you end up just like old Uncle Billy. Shame."

"Seriously."

"I'm watching," Billy said, looking at the girl. "I see everything. I know where that puck's going before the carrier does. Did you forget who taught you this game? You can't wish all that away just because you and everyone else voted old Uncle Billy off the Christmas list."

H stood and lifted the car seat and put himself between Jo and Billy.

"Hey," Billy said. "We were talking."

"Your fawning is making everybody uncomfortable."

Billy gestured at the empty bleachers. "Which everybody?"

"Exactly," H said.

"Exactly," Billy said.

On the ice, the boys were getting crisscrossed and threaded by this team from San Jose. H put his hands in the pockets of his Carhartt and, though he felt nothing, he remembered that he'd stowed the pistol in the compartment along the lining at his ribs. Slipping the gun into the jacket each morning went something like dropping a contact lens into the eye: blink a few times, then everything goes clear. He noticed the gun's absence, not its presence. When he wore the wrong coat, he felt unprepared, as if he'd gone without brushing his teeth or without taking a cup of coffee. But carry, and he could speak and stand tall and rise and meet the world, rather than slouch through.

Coach had replaced him in the lineup with a kid named Spinella, who was seventeen and who snapped around the ice like lightning cracking, hunted the puck like a bloodhound, and showed no fear at—seemed to express delight about—putting a shoulder into a defender twice his size. The newer model, H thought, innovated and improved. H's face had healed, leaving the skin around his eye darkened but whole. He was beginning to look like a citizen again.

The puck went for an icing and the referee called the play dead.

"What's with this goalie?" Billy said.

"Which?"

"Guy must be freezing out there. Hey, wrong sport, buddy."

"Jesus, Billy."

"I'm just saying, the kid's got to be six foot six. Are you trying to tell me that nobody nowhere needed a point guard?"

"What century is this?"

"They've already got basketball, football, half of baseball. Can't we keep anything the way it was? Why's everybody got to have a point to prove?"

"It's not zero-sum, Billy. You understand what that means? It's not either-or."

"Take a joke, son. Don't be so sensitive. A guy can't even talk around your generation without first having to apologize for taking a breath. It's not like I'm asking for him to drink from a different fountain. And, anyway, it *is* zero-sum, or are you sitting up here for the view?"

"I'm sitting up here because they found someone better."

"This kid, ninety-seven? This string bean?"

"His name's Spinella. He comes from Tucson or Tulsa or some place in the center of the country, which, apparently, now has hockey. Watch him go to space." H folded the blanket down against Jo's chin. "Watch him find lanes. He's a stride ahead of the others, not so much in how he skates but in where he skates. The play comes to him."

"Kid can't seem to catch a pass, can he?"

"He's nervous," H said. "That's jitters. That'll calm. It takes a few games, but it'll calm."

"He's coughed up the puck three times in as many shifts."

"It's nerves. His fundamentals are tight. Look at how he moves out there. He's got the puck where he wants it in one, two touches. He's got three-hundred-and-sixty-degree awareness. Watch this kid backcheck."

On the ice, the Spinella kid curled low behind the net,

received a pass, turned and fired. Each action occurred like a flourish, like how a rich man signs a check: without lifting the pen.

"The nerves will pass," H said. "All it takes is one big hit. One good shot that knocks the snot out of you, that literally knocks the snot from your nose. You taste blood on your tongue and on your canines. You go from running scared to on the prowl."

Spinella hustled off the ice as fast as he'd leapt on. He sat, and Coach gave him something like a smack, a pat, on the shoulder. H thought he could feel the touch on his own skin.

"Something about that pain—the first fight, the first big hit, whatever—that blasts the fear from you. Strange how that works, isn't it? The fear goes as soon as you feel pain. Or remember it. It's never so bad as it seems. Believe me, this kid's going to be something."

"I found our boy, H."

"Spinella?"

"Who's Spinella? Williams. I found Ben Williams." Billy leaned over and took the lid from H's drink and, producing a flask, he poured a measure of booze in over the soda. He returned the canteen to his jacket pocket. "You're not going to like what I learned."

"Put it to rest, Billy."

"You ought to see the truck he drives. You ought to see the gig he's got."

"I'm not interested in the truck he drives. I've got other things to worry about."

"Do you still have the G-U-N?"

H shrugged his shoulders to shift the revolver inside his

coat. Hadn't he just carried his daughter into this building? How could both be true? He looked at Billy. "What is it you think is going to happen? Tell me what picture you have in your head."

Billy leaned in, eyes still on the ice, and whispered. "You follow him around a bit, find the right moment, then *pow*." He made his fingers into a pistol. "You know, *finito*. Gonzo. That old story."

"I threw that gun away. Do you understand? Grow up. Come down to planet Earth, already. Sarah's fine. She's healed, and she's clean, and she put that whole mess behind her. She's on with her life."

"You think I'm doing this for Sarah?" Billy snorted. "This has got nothing to do with her. This has everything to do with a piece-of-shit scumbag who goes away for a blink and comes out free and clean, comes home to a truck and the pay to match, with time and a half on the weekends. You're up here in the stands, and that criminal, meanwhile, is walking free, a danger to himself and the community. You got any idea what they do to child molesters in prison? If you think he was unhinged before, Jesus, imagine what he's capable of now."

"Sarah wasn't a child. She was fifteen."

"You defend him? Am I hearing right? How about looking at yourself, then? How about that?"

"I'm busy, Billy. I've got a life. I've got rent due. Get your head out of your ass. Nobody cares anymore but you. There's nothing that man can offer me."

"Not a zero-sum game, is that it?"

"Exactly that, Billy. That's exactly it."

"You know, I remember your first game with these guys. You were out at that rink in Portland. Do you remember? Your knees were knocking during the national anthem. I thought you were going to drop your stick you were shaking so badly."

"I relaxed."

"You sure did, H. You popped a goal early in the second, didn't you? You put a hell of a move on that defender, twisted him all up, and picked exactly your corner of the net. Goaltender never stood a chance."

"It was a lucky shot."

"H, tell me something. On your deathbed, will we all have to lean in just to hear you say, 'Sorry, sorry, so sorry.' Is that the idea?"

"I didn't ask you to sit here."

"You think all these years on this team were an accident? You think I don't know any better?" Billy brought a plastic cup to his lip and spat a jet of tobacco. "I've been watching you on the ice since you were four years old, remember? I'm the one who bought you your first pair of skates. Do you remember that?"

"I was there, Billy."

"That's right. I was there too. Think your old man cared about this game? Think your mom knew any better? I taught you to play. I'm the one who stayed out with you, skating under streetlights or out on the pond before dark. I know what sort of player you are. What do you think it does to me watching you here, benched, while these kids take your shot? Think this is fair?"

"Watch him move, Bill. I've got nothing left to say to a kid like that."

"Jesus, H, I can't hear the game over the sound of your nonsense."

"Which is?"

"Which is that you could skate circles around this kid or that one. Huh? Go watch the footage for yourself, you don't believe me. If this coach has some problem with you, that's fine, but don't scorch everything that came before him. You could play. The only thing you never did was take your talent seriously. Any halfway-decent coach would have seen that and would have talked to you and developed you into the top-rate skater you were meant to be. Instead, here you are, replaced by some kid from Tucson, and all you want to do is apologize about it, pretend like everything's your fault and so sorry to interrupt. Like fair's fair."

"And it's not?"

"Goddamn it, H, it's not. Goddamn it, they're eating your lunch. They've got their hands in your pockets. Where's your girl? Where's your job? Where's your family? Where's your money? Where's your degree? Who's going to care for this kid? How you going to feed your daughter? How many shifts do you plan to drive tomorrow? I've got no reason to lie to you, son. I haven't got the years left for anything but the truth. You could play, and this coach and that team and your girl, wherever she is, left you. Not the other way around. You are stuck with a bill you didn't rack up. How many ways do I have to say it? Now, will you please grow up, and please have a drink already."

Billy offered the flask again. H looked to Jo. Was there an edge to be softened? All wrong. A man can do both. A man can do all three, four, five. Christine had whipped herself into a frenzy, had conjured up a monster, called it parenting, then retreated. He'd known her his whole life: people who needed an enemy, who existed in opposition only. Place the counterpoint first so you know where to stand. Careened through life, these women and these men did, with fists clenched and swinging. H wouldn't say that what Christine was feeling was all in her head, but he knew that he could get this girl fed and changed and to sleep at night and home safe at the end of a day, starting with this one. Seemed like 101. Whatever for was all this fuss?

H brought his hands from his pockets. "Think so?"

"I know it. Tell me you don't."

H took a drink.

EIGHT

The kid at the door stood from his stool. He had a tablet in one hand and offered the other. H held Jo's carrier in his right, so he twisted and shook with the left.

"Murray," H said.

"You're getting to be our number one customer."

"Here I thought we were colleagues."

Murray bent and waved to the baby. "Little Jo, you menace. Look what you do to your pop."

Jo sucked on her pacifier. She'd just woken from a nap, and her eyes were fixed forward and her pupils were dilated.

"How's the wait?" H asked.

Murray looked at his computer. "Ten, fifteen minutes. Not so bad. We are a machine these days: angry drivers come in, happy drivers go out. Elena's working."

"Anything from your sister?" H said.

"All good, H. She came home. She's like nothing happened. She doesn't say where she went, but she's talking, playing video games, cooking, eating. My mom's relieved."

"We were all teenagers once."

"Sure, H, but I never ran off. I just played video games and felt alone all the time."

"Were we supposed to grow out of that?"

Murray smiled. "H, you've got to try the new coffee."

"It's good?"

"It's shit, but it's new."

"I thought this company had billions of dollars. I open up any newspaper, and all I read about is your boy-genius founder."

"Valued at," Murray said. "This company is *valued at* billions. Big difference, amigo."

"Once I studied economics."

"Guess who does the valuing. The investors! How about that? The guys that put in the money get to say how much the company's worth. Bonkers, right? Sixty-eight billion for them. We get watery coffee."

"It's new, though."

"And free," Murray said. "Make yourself comfortable."

H took Jo and sat. Folding chairs and outdated magazines and a carpet that had been worn thin made the room seem like a place where you waited to get your teeth drilled. The air smelled recycled, laced, maybe with oxygen, like at a mall or a casino. Television screens looped advertisements for banks, cheap cell phone plans, dollar stores, and subprime auto loans. Blue light went from screens to ceilings to walls to the cheeks and eyes of the men who sat waiting.

Murray had returned to his stool, and as he waited to greet drivers, he put the tablet on his thighs and watched traffic move down Route 1. Across the room, Elena and another staff member that H didn't recognize worked the counter. The drivers—all men—sat waiting for their turn to be seen. One, in a T-shirt and a pair of jeans and Timberland boots, wore his cap low over his eyes and nodded to the music in his headphones. Others were dressed as if for a job interview: young Haitians and Jamaicans wearing suits or jackets, jewelry, and shirts stiff with starch. No one else was white. Most slept or sat curled over their phones. They and H amounted to an operating expense a year or two from being mitigated. They were a dent in the bottom line. Somewhere, in a boardroom, kids from Kellogg Business School were analyzing the situation: we've got this taxi company with a driver problem. One day, a ribbon would be cut, and a fleet of automated cars or hover-pods would come rolling forth. H and the others would no longer be needed. This space could once again be used for handing out food stamps or for drawing predatory loans against Medicaid credits.

Jo had fallen back asleep. Her lips, latched to her sucker, twitched. In her mother's absence, she'd begun to behave as if she were looking after H. She kept quiet, asked for little, and seemed to regard him with patience. He wondered whatever had so upset Christine.

At the counter, a Hispanic guy, short and midsixties, stood clutching his car keys. A rosary dangled from his other hand, and he twitched his wrist to wind and unwind the beads around two fingers like a lifeguard with a whistle. At the second desk, two guys wearing different colored tracksuits leaned on their elbows. One translated for the other from what sounded like French, maybe Creole. Elena and her partner never looked up from their computers. They nodded and typed and gave smiles that were meant to communicate shared suffering: "It pains us to see you so, brother," and, "Let's see how we can help."

H knew the staff was authorized to deliver only the message from the mother ship. And the rub was always the same: you pay, we collect. Drivers came in to sort out some trouble with their checks, to work some angle to get back on the road or paid more or faster, but everything seemed to resolve in service of the machine. Here came the bill, H thought, and those three—in their tracksuits, with their prayer beads—have zero days left to pay. In a cloud somewhere, in a server farm in the Pacific Ocean, a string of code written by some teenager selected who lived and who died and who got to gobble up all the money and youth. H felt like a man waiting for a noose to free up.

He stood and brewed himself something called Island Blend, which came sputtering from the machine tepid. Overhead, speakers played the same classic rock that had been on the radio for the last hundred years: Elton John, Eric Clapton, John Mellencamp.

When they called his name, H brought Jo to the desk, and Elena leaned forward and served a smile.

"Jesus, fuck, H," she said. "What are you doing to me? Put her up here already."

"She's half asleep," H said, setting his daughter in her carrier on the countertop.

"That bow," Elena said. "Jesus. Hi," she said to the baby. "I love you. You're perfect."

"Say hello."

As if on cue, Jo blinked and pursed her lips.

"Ugh, H, you are not good-looking enough to create this angel on your own. Her mother must be a movie star. Okay," the girl said. "I quit. What more do I need from this life?"

"Don't quit before you fix my account."

"I can't keep bailing you out, H. My agita." She typed to pull open his account. "Your pop," she said to Jo, "has a very hard time playing by the very simple rules. Here, see," she said. "Your account's deactivated again. Guess who reported you." Elena snapped a piece of bubble gum.

"There was a woman. I took her to a bridge game. She sat in the back and didn't say anything about Jo, which seemed strange because she watched her the whole ride."

"Marion Peterson," Elena said. "No, she gave you five stars. It was a kid: Chris Marks. You've driven him a few times around the Seaport."

"That kid?" H said. "I thought we were pals."

"He reported you."

"Snakes, Elena. This city writhes. Can you clean it up for me?"

She was fussing around in the computer, and a crease formed across her brow. "H," she said.

"What's up?"

"Oh, H. Poor H. They've got you flagged as having a defective vehicle."

"It's the same car as always."

"Your car is registered with four belts, but when you ride around with the baby, you've only got three. It's the third report in a week. We've got a policy. H, they're not going to let you drive around with Jo. They're just not. It's against the rules."

"Good thing they're opening a daycare, is that it?"

"I'm sorry, H. But three strikes plus your record—there's nothing I can do."

"What about my record?"

"You submitted to a background check when you applied

to drive, remember? I can see your police record. Anybody in the system can see."

"Did I agree to that?" H tried to remember filling out the paperwork. He was sure he'd given them everything, that he'd checked some box that told them to take whatever they wanted. Fine print like twenty-first-century poetry: all our bards were tech lawyers, and all they wanted was your soul.

"I can see it here," she said, tapping the screen. "What'd you do, anyway?"

"Nothing. A misunderstanding. That was a lifetime ago, and it was supposed to come off my record, anyway. Can't you do something for me? I've got rent. I've got—" He paused. "I've got her."

"H, you and me are the same. I'm a temp. I'm a nursing student earning shitty minimum wage for some company that doesn't even know my name. They don't trust me to fix anything real."

"What about Murray?"

"Nobody here has permissions. Three strikes go up to headquarters in California. They've got a file open on you now with the security team. H, honey. They aren't going to let you drive, not with the baby. Listen," she said, looking up from the computer. "Here's what you do: go sign up with the other guys, then whenever you need to drive, call me up, and I'll babysit this one for you, no charge. The other service is just like ours. Some guys say they even make more money there."

"Shit, Elena. I need to drive today."

"I'm sorry, H," she said. "It's shitty, I know. I wish I could do something."

Shifting his weight, H felt the pistol in its pocket against his ribs, and a shiver passed from the small of his back to his shoulders, then to the tips of his fingers.

"Listen, thanks," he told Elena. "I appreciate your help. I really do."

"They'll email you as soon as they have a ruling. I'll send good thoughts."

"Don't waste them," H said, and he waved and took Jo and left.

Outside, he found the Haitian in the tracksuit smoking a cigarette. The translator had gone. The afternoon was soggy, and overhead, a lump of atmosphere swelled and threatened to split open. H nodded hello. He felt the dampness in his joints.

"They tossed you too?" the guy asked.

"You speak English?"

The guy grinned, flashing teeth white like the center of the sun.

"Why pretend?"

He tilted his head from one side to the other. "Maybe get some sympathy. Maybe make it seem like, you know, I need the job."

"Don't you?"

The guy laughed. "I fell asleep while driving." He laughed again. "Oops."

"They closed your account."

The guy was done with his cigarette, and he tossed it to the pavement, where it landed in a puddle. "I got lots of jobs. I don't drive for them, I can drive for the competitor. I can do anything I want. I'm not afraid of them. Did they toss you?"

"I've been doing this for fun," H said. "I'm a hockey player. This is for spending cash, you know? I don't really need it."

The guy nodded. "You should try Errand," he said.

"Errand?"

"Just like this." The guy held up his phone. "Get a ping, go fetch rich people's clothes, walk their dogs, pick up their groceries. Simple shit. No drunk kids. No gas money. Don't have to keep the car clean. Do your own thing and make money just as good."

H wanted to take the gun, to set down Jo's carrier and instead hold the weapon and take into his lungs the air off Highway 1, where hubcaps came tottering from speeding cars and the smell of fast food and exhaust mingled with the saltwater breeze from Revere Beach. Jo gurgled.

"They don't care how you dress." The guy nodded toward Jo. "They don't care if you have a kid or whatever. It's good."

H put his hand in his pocket. "Errand."

"That's the one, friend." The man fixed a baseball cap onto his brow. "Errand for now. Tomorrow, some teenager invents something new: Fetch, maybe. Get-My-Shit. Who knows? I'm not picky."

H nodded. "I'll look into it."

The guy pointed. "You got vomit on your shoulder."

H twisted to find the stain. "Shit. Thanks."

The guy smiled, then crossed the lot to where four dogs were leashed to a handicap parking sign. He knelt and untied them, and H smiled. Walker? PetPal? Every one of these companies had a name like for a line of toys. As the guy walked off, towing the fleet of pups behind him, he offered a wave, which H returned.

NINE

The phone rang and woke Jo, who gasped, taking a breath about the size of her universe, as if what she wanted to say were equal to everything else she knew. And then she was hollering. We know this pain, don't we?

H had Jo strapped into a carrier that he wore like a vest. She seemed sensitive to his moods these days, but she'd become delicate too. Regular stimuli—a phone ringing, the flash of a camera—caused stress that seemed to prick her like a pin. She cried her anger.

The bulldog H was walking, in response to Jo's fit, sat and started licking itself. Each time H retrieved this thing from its owner's apartment, there was some new designer treat waiting on the counter: baked goods, canned French foods, strips of dried animal meat. The dog lived better than H did, which it seemed to know, and in response it treated each walk like an extravaganza. Every fire hydrant was sniffed. Every tree got sprayed. It couldn't pass a stoop without climbing and barking at somebody's front door. "This creature," H would say to Jo as they walked, "represents all the reasons I'll ever tell you no—not because I don't love you, not because I wouldn't give you every last thing. Look at this pooch and understand how come we can't get what we want."

Now, the bulldog sat, and Jo cried, and the phone kept ringing. The other two pups—the mutt with half an ear missing and the one that looked part teddy bear—tugged forward, pulling him in as many directions at once. H pawed around his pocket until he found a sucker, which he gave to Jo. She went quiet. He answered.

"Christine," H said.

"Andrew."

"Ah, Christ." He swung the phone around to his other ear and cradled it with his shoulder. "Sarah, I've got about zero seconds right now."

Jo spat her pacifier to the sidewalk. Two of the dogs lurched, but H crouched and snatched it from the brick before they could. The fences in this neighborhood were made of cast iron. The roads were cobblestone. Every rowhouse had a garden. Every paint job was high gloss. He and Jo were tourists, aliens.

"Is that her?" Sarah asked.

H stood and put the sucker into his own mouth to clean it, then gave it back to the girl. "I've got to go, Sarah. I'm busy. Stop calling me, would you?"

"I was thinking about you," she said, going on as she did, without listening to a word he told her. "I saw you with Billy at the game the other night."

She could have this conversation with a wall. Which made H wonder, If my half doesn't mean a fucking thing, then why doesn't she do her part alone?

"Stop coming already. Don't you have a life to see to?"

"Remember that rink at Loomis?" she said. "The one that was half outdoors. We'd freeze watching you play. I'd dress for a blizzard."

"I don't really remember, Sarah. I was a kid."

"Dad would buy me hot chocolate. We'd fill into that warming room, which was always overstuffed with parents in puffy coats and me and Dad and Billy. I must have been twelve, thirteen then. Of all the rinks we followed you to, that one charmed me the most."

Still shouldering the phone, he bundled the leashes in his left hand and gave the pups a tug. The stupid one crouched to shit. A woman, midfifties, in sagging yoga pants, power-walked past with elbows up, wearing headphones the size of softballs over both ears.

"All my early memories of you are from rinks," Sarah said. "I don't remember your first steps, but I do remember you learning to skate. Isn't that something?"

"A treasure."

"It was so odd to see you sitting. And sitting with Uncle Billy of all people."

"We can't all turn our backs and plug our ears, can we? We can't just put him out on the iceberg and push."

"Billy knows where to find me. And he'd be welcome."

"And Dad?"

"Dad would say the same thing. If Billy is on his own, it's not for our lack of trying. Nothing would make me happier than to reconcile."

"You've got some way of remembering only the good bits, huh? All our glasses are half empty, and you're drinking straight from the tap."

"The whole world didn't freeze in place ten years ago, H. There's a present history for you to remember and a present moment for you to live in—if you're interested."

"I guess we're just talking past each other. Sorry to let you down."

She clicked her tongue. "H, you couldn't, could you? You've got steel wool for guts. You were hardened by fire."

"Sarah, I'm in the middle of about a million things."

The baby cried out.

"There's my niece," Sarah said. "I can hear her."

"They can hear her on the space station."

The dog finished shitting, and H yanked the leashes to lead the animals on. Somebody passing started a fuss about the mess, wanting to know if H planned to leave it there. Sometimes there weren't enough hands to tell the world how you felt. H pulled forward.

"I watched you the whole game, and I wondered just what Uncle Billy wanted you to know so badly. Strange to see you two together. He doesn't look well, sitting hunched over like that. His posture's gone crooked. He doesn't resemble the man I remember. I thought of coming over, but then there was something unnatural about it."

"You and me talking?"

"Sitting with you at a hockey rink, instead of sitting to watch you. I guess you would have had to grow out of it someday, but that's just not how I like to think of you. I prefer to keep you frozen still, wrapped up like silverware hidden away in the linen closet."

"I was cut, Sarah," he said. "I didn't grow out of it."

She sighed, which made her sound, to his ear, something

like an adult, like their mother. What, he wondered, did she look like these days, if time had so ravaged the rest of them? Had the weight returned? Had her hair grown long? Did her skin still shimmer like melting ice, or did she have that pinkness that she'd had as a girl, before she'd done everything short of pull a trigger trying to kill herself and everybody else?

"Is there anything in particular that you need, Sarah?"

"I wanted to tell you that the twins have started talking," she said.

"Why?"

"They bubble, H. They just bubble."

"I mean, why did you want to tell me that? What makes you think I care to know?"

"Cole looks like Dad, which is to say he looks like you. I feel born for it, H. Is that how it happened with you? Is that how you feel? Everything I've ever done seems only a warm-up, only practice for parenthood. Do you know what I mean?"

"So glad we could be of service."

"Of course, that's to say that I love you for it. I love this, and so I love you for preparing me for it."

"I wish like hell, Sarah, that you just wouldn't."

"How can I not?"

He tugged on the bulldog to get the thing moving. A few blocks away, in a brownstone with a yellow door, with flower boxes on every window, this dog had a bed with its name stenciled on it.

"Hey, Sarah."

"Yes, H."

"Stop calling me. Seriously. I don't have shit to say. What

I do have are full hands and empty pockets. So just give me a break, why don't you?"

"You don't have to pick up," she said. "But you do. You always answer, and I know why."

"Because I think you're someone else calling? Because I press the wrong button?"

"Because you want to be a family again."

"Live on whatever planet makes you happiest. That's fine. But leave me out of it. I'm not mad at you. I'm not mad at little Cole and Melissa. I don't care about Neil and his promotions and his money and his cars and his philanthropy—least of all, his philanthropy. I care as much about that as I care about astrophysics and vegan diets. And as for your kids, no offense, I hope they're healthy, I hope they've started talking, and I hope they stay somebody else's problem and never my own."

"You answer, H, because you want to forgive me. It's not in your nature to be so angry. You're too good. I remember how you cared for me for all those years. How you covered for me and picked me up from parties and lied to Mom and Dad to try to keep me out of trouble. You were always the one."

The bulldog was now growling at the mutt, making like it wanted a fight that both H and the other dog knew it didn't. Suddenly it started yelping, and then, there went Jo again, screaming.

"Christ," he said.

With the baby crying and the dogs circling and barking, Sarah said, "Christine called."

"Perfect." H tied the bulldog's leash around a city bench and brought the other two to the park. The bulldog started howling.

"She thought she'd done something wrong," Sarah said.

"That her feelings made her some sort of monster. You know that's not the case, don't you?"

"What a treat it is for me that you two have found each other."

"I felt that way too," Sarah said. "It's a strange and unnatural feeling, but it's also a miracle: you can't have the kids close enough, and you can't get far enough from them. You feel like having them there is somehow a loss. Of course, what you're actually experiencing is something like crossed wires, emotions triggered by chemical imbalances. It's normal. Some of us are preconditioned to experience motherhood this way. I told her it passes. She needs to speak to someone—a doctor. I told her so. I also made sure she knew that she'd learn to love being a mother and that she'd never imagine a time when she hadn't. I think you're doing the right thing by giving her space."

"Christine takes what Christine wants. I follow behind as best I can."

Sarah laughed. "That's part of why I like her so much. She feels terrible, you know, H. She feels like a terrible person. But what she's done is brave and so hard. Is there anything more difficult than admitting you have a problem? You should call her. I think she's waiting for you to call."

Once inside the fence, H unlatched the two dogs, and they started tearing around the park, sniffing, barking, chasing the other animals. Across the street, the bulldog stared as if unable to fathom the snub.

"Stay out of it," H said. "Can you do me that favor? And since you've already got your mind made up, I have been calling. Every day. Every one. She wants to talk about swimming laps for some charity. She can tell me all about knitting scarves for the homeless. And she has not a thing—not one—to say about this baby, her family, or coming home."

Some neighbor crouched next to the bulldog and started scratching the thing behind the ears. The woman looked around for an owner, with a frown creasing her face, as if she couldn't imagine who'd leave such an angel tied up to a bench. What monster, she seemed to want to know. H took his daughter's foot between his fingers and squeezed. The woman read the dog's tags and went for her phone.

"If that's so, it's only because she's ashamed," Sarah said. "She needs you, H."

"I have to go," H said.

"Step up, H. Take care of her. You have to be the bigger person. I know what you have to give. I remember."

"As interesting as all this is, Sarah, I have to go. Don't call me anymore."

"You know I will. Just like I know that you'll answer."

"Whatever you say, Sarah. Isn't that always it?" He hung up the phone and took Jo across the street.

"That's mine," he said to the lady. "That's my dog."

Without standing, the woman turned her eyes upon him and studied the sight: this bruised, damaged kid and his baby daughter. "You shouldn't leave him tied up like this." The lady said. "It's cruel."

"He's a little shit," H told her. "He deserves a bit of cruelty."

The woman gasped.

"Don't fret, lady. We'll build him some character yet. Every sinner's got a future, haven't they?"

The woman glared.

"And every saint has a past, for that matter."

She stood, pulled her coat closed around her neck, and then stormed off as if he'd just trampled over her azaleas. The bulldog woofed.

"Keep it down," H said to the animal. "You speak when spoken to." He was still holding his phone, and he saw, there, among his contacts, collecting dust, Billy's number, right next to Christine's: B then C. He dialed.

TEN

Mist dampened the pavement of his city. H sat in a wheelchair he'd found collapsed near the ticket booth for a harbor cruise. Jo slept in her stroller beside him. An overhang sheltered them from the weather. The pistol was in his pocket.

H sipped coffee from a Styrofoam cup, and with a foot, he rocked the carriage to keep Jo still and asleep. She'd been up on the hour, every hour, last night, giving him all hell, crying aloud everything she felt about him and his parenting.

Beyond the yacht, which bobbed in its berth behind him, and from over the airport, dawn lifted and caromed through the bay, setting water adazzle with light and shadow. Above, gulls circled and cawed. Higher still, rumbled the engines of planes rising from or descending into Logan. H counted three construction sites on this block: to his left a new hotel, then a tower of condominiums, and then ahead, spanning a stretch of Congress Street, the new Goldman building. A dive bar he'd been to before he met Christine had been reduced to rubble and mud. Rat traps punctuated the sidewalk. Construction had chopped up the roads and left potholes. Everything would be new, would have private balconies and luxury finishes and concierge services, but everything, now, was in flux, designed but not delivered, payoffs yet unrealized.

Ahead, the site for a new tower was a hole that gaped four stories down. According to Billy, the crew, which hadn't yet arrived, included a bunch of union guys and Benjamin Williams.

A street man worked his way up the sidewalk, stooping now and then to pluck cigarette butts from cracks in the cement. A city bus, empty and yellow, rolled past with a hiss. Across the street, a girl inside a Dunkin' Donuts was unfurling rubber mats, laying them over tile to make a path from the door to the counter. Her hijab was the same pink as the *D* in the store sign. In the window of a boutique gym, which spanned the second floor of a new condominium, a woman bobbed on a treadmill and appeared as a silhouette, dark against yellow light. H smelled bagels baking. A cyclist in black spandex—face covered in some sort of space-age balaclava—thudded over snow and broken cement in the direction of the brewery. A Coca-Cola truck pulled over at a deli, and a man in coveralls and work gloves and a ball cap came out, chattering into an earpiece as he unloaded cases of soda onto a handcart.

After five thirty, traffic on the roads quickened. By six, workers began to arrive. Pickups with empty payloads came on-site and parked, and men in sweatshirts and safety vests and hard hats emerged, smoking, sipping coffee from paper cups.

They rubbed their eyes with gloved hands. They left their trucks for other vehicles, which rattled into action: a Cat, a forklift, a pile driver, a food truck. An American flag the size of a jumbo jet flapped from the neck of a crane. A cop came and parked his cruiser and sat in the driver's seat and monitored traffic. H watched.

A red Ford pickup arrived. Yellow-and-white lettering on the door said *Williams and Sons Construction.* H stood. The truck turned on-site. Then, H was already crossing the street, was already clutching the chain-link fence, had left Jo there sleeping in her stroller.

H watched the truck park. The door opened and Williams came forth—very tall, very broad, black skin, black hair worn close to his skull, face shaved clean. He wore a tool belt on his shoulder. He seemed alert.

H knew and recognized nothing about this man. He remembered nothing about Benjamin Williams. The face, this person, was strange to H. He could have been anyone.

A car horn honked. H turned. He'd left his child alone in a stroller on the sidewalk by the 7-Eleven in cold April weather. H rushed back and took her in his arms. As they walked to the car, Jo was silent.

———————

On Saturdays, H followed Williams to the parking lot at the Micro Center. Williams crossed Memorial Drive on foot, then began jogging. He started early and moved at a clip that left other runners behind.

Williams ran through Harvard, across the river, and into and around the football stadium: up one row, over, then down the next. He ran until he'd completed a full cycle, then took a knee and touched the grass. From end zone to end zone he trotted, knees high, jerking sometimes, as if to avoid a defender. He jumped and slapped the upright of the far goalpost, then, without breaking, Williams returned to the Esplanade and jogged to the outdoor gym near the BU boathouse. On the chin-up bar, he performed one hundred pull-ups in sets of twenty. He did two hundred sit-ups in sets of forty. With feet dangling above him, like a contortionist, a circus act, he did push-ups vertically. Partway through the routine each morning, Williams removed his sweatshirt and worked, then, in only a tank top. His arms pulsed. His shoulders swelled. He went alone, drank water from the public fountain, spat, and took no rest. When he finished at the gym, he began again to run: down past the Hatch Shell, the Museum of Science, the police station, back into Cambridge by the boatyard. He tiptoed around goose shit as if threading through a defensive line. He ran the boardwalk near the kayaks, and those ancient boards beneath him padded.

To keep pace, H brought a ten-speed he'd once taken from his parents' garage. He bought some contraption from a bike shop in Allston that was waterproof, windproof, and shaded and that let him tow Jo behind him on half-sized tires. When Williams paused at the outdoor gym, H parked his bike and checked on the girl and found her face curled in delight, pink gums clamping and arms flailing for more. She wanted speed. She delighted in motion. Sometimes as they rode, she fell asleep. Always keeping pace with Williams proved difficult. A few weeks ago, H had been a semiprofessional athlete. But this man dragged H through the park on legs that looked like tree trunks but moved like a dancer's.

At the end of the loop, H watched from the parking lot of the Whole Foods, gasping. Williams dressed, took from the truck a bottle of water to which he added some sort of powder, shook, and drank. If the sludge trickled down his cheeks, Williams wiped his face with the back of his wrist. He wore no headphones. He spoke to no one.

At seven thirty on Saturday mornings, Williams got into his pickup and left.

———————

On Thursday evenings, Williams went to a bar nestled in among the row houses near BU Medical. The place served burgers and pints of beer to hipsters and to the blue-collar townies, who looked ragged from trying to weather the gentrification. Jazz musicians came to blow horns, rake snares, or pluck a stand-up bass. Men and women set up their own instruments on a stage atop of which was laid a red oriental rug. The walls were brick, and the tables were set in against one another. A bartender with tits like zeppelins waited on customers, serving smiles, serving looks down her tank top. Williams behaved, kept his eyes up, and only ever mumbled his order as if speaking to the tabletop before him. The bartender winked and pointed to his Coke and asked if Williams wanted something harder.

He always shook his head no, said thanks, and like a monk, returned to the book he was reading: Chomsky's lectures, 1963 to 2013. H searched Chomsky online. He hadn't gotten very far before he dropped out. He couldn't make sense of the man's biography.

When the waitress came to H's table, she'd offer a compliment and a pair of pursed lips for the baby. When she asked what he'd have, H ordered a drink, shocked, as always, at what a beer cost in some parts of the city. But he ordered one anyway and nursed the thing. The baby, despite the noise, stayed quiet. H draped a blanket over the top of her carrier to keep her still. She could be loyal. She'd been paying attention. H began to wonder how much of this fuss was all in her mother's imagination.

Williams ordered a hamburger, red and bloody, and cut it in two before he ate. He took salad on the side, held his book folded over its own snapped spine, and read quickly. When the act started, he'd dog-ear the page, pocket the paperback, and turn his attention to the band. He listened through to the first intermission. Then the singer sometimes would go out for a smoke. The band might get a pint at the bar. Williams paid cash for his tab without asking for it, packed his things, went to the restroom, and left.

Most mornings Williams went to mass. The chapel, H could see from the street, was small: a dozen pews, a piano, a choir, families and children and men and women praying with raised hands. The priest had dark skin and coiffed hair and a reedy voice that delivered sermons half in song.

Some evenings Williams returned to that same church for meetings. Alcoholics, drug addicts, sex addicts, and who knew what else, broke after an hour to smoke cigarettes on the sidewalk. They flicked butts into the street. They came out drinking coffee. Their arms were thin, stringy, muscled, and tattooed, or they had bellies, thick and round, that bulged from behind untucked T-shirts. Everyone had combed their hair up tight, like altar boys, as if to advertise their sorrow.

Some mornings music could be heard from inside the

church. Some nights the sound of applause came through open windows. When these men and women and Williams left the chapel, they did so single file. They said nothing to one another—"not goodbye," not "see you next time." They broke for their cars and trucks. They returned to their lives. H watched them and thought of TV dinners, sagging couches, basement apartments. He watched from the front seat of his car parked in a corner of the lot. When Williams left, H followed him back to his house, which was on the second floor of a triple-decker in Roxbury near the park. Williams left his truck on the street, then entered through a back door. The place was dark when he arrived, but then on came a kitchen light, and then the blue flash of a television.

H stayed and watched until the baby fussed, and then he brought her home and cared for her and bathed her and put her in new clothes, and a fresh diaper. He combed her sweet hair. He read her a book. When he closed her bedroom door, she cried and wailed for her mother. He listened from the other side of the wall with his face in his hands. All of this seemed so cruel.

Eventually she screamed herself into exhaustion. She would go quiet. She would sleep. In the mornings, when she woke, she greeted him fresh, bearing no signs of the trauma she'd expressed the night before. What should he make of her fury, of her forgetting? What was she trying to tell him? He dressed his daughter. He readied them for the day.

ELEVEN

Up came the Seaport—how many skyscrapers, how many condos—to form a Boston part two, a Boston for the rich, by the rest of us. Williams worked this boom. With a pen stroke, the mayor had tipped the funnel of money. He'd invited all his favorite developers to build a new city right next to the existing one. And these barons couldn't invest fast enough, couldn't bake a pie too big, cut only the fattest slices for themselves and all their children. Most mornings, as H sat and watched Williams, the city sounded like a motor running, like lips being licked, like cash registers opening and closing. Want a place downtown? Come up with $800, $900—even a $1,000—a square foot. Who had it? The Saudis. Chinese heirs and heiresses. Shell companies and LLCs. That same mayor had named this swath the Innovation District. Giant scissors snapped at ribbon cuttings. Champagne was popped. Innovation? Put some money in, take out much more. Call it an incubator for a retirement fund, a graveyard for a way of living, a tax haven with four different dog bakeries.

H had tried to get work on these construction crews but had found them insular. Everybody knew a guy who knew a guy who knew a guy, and anyway, H didn't have a single skill. He couldn't swing a hammer, couldn't push a wheelbarrow. Once this sort of work had been done by alcoholics from Lynn and Lowell, by guys with short fuses and troubled marriages and children who would take SAT prep courses and go on to study liberal arts. H knew these men. He'd played hockey with their kids. Were they still in charge, he might have found work here. But now, every crew spoke more Spanish than English. Everybody looked like Williams, like they came from Dorchester or Roxbury. They dressed differently. They played music H didn't know. They were black and brown or something in between, and they behaved as if they had keys to one another's garages, as if they'd all gone to the same quinceañera the weekend before.

Before Jo was born, Christine insisted he apply for these jobs. They went to the library and spent two hours reformatting his résumé. She was seven months pregnant and had to get up to piss every twenty minutes. When they finished, they printed out three dozen copies and spent hours delivering them to construction sites around the city. They should have saved the paper. No one replied. H signed up to drive instead.

Now, seeing these crews, H wondered, were he somebody's cousin, were he dating somebody's niece, would they have called? H remembered the truck: Williams and Sons. These men hadn't played on H's peewee hockey team, they'd shot hoops at Basketball City, played intertown league out of Roxbury. Maybe Williams had been their point guard, had had a mother who brought orange slices for halftime. Williams pushed a broom around a cement slab, flossed mud from the teeth of an excavator, and H registered privilege, saw opportunity un-earned. The currency was the same, it'd simply been greased into different palms.

Above, a crane was raising and setting framework. Steel beams, lifted and dangling, were placed and welded put. A sign zip-tied to the chain-link fence said, "Luxury condos coming spring 2020! Half leased and going fast!" Someone in a polo shirt on a boat somewhere off the Cape had already made his money. And even Williams—for smoking a cigarette now and then, for flattening a plot of tar, for leaning on the knob of a shovel, and despite the assault, the record, his sentence—got paid too.

Jo, from the stroller, watched with amazement. The trucks, the engines, the seagulls, the planes—all this clatter seemed to awe and captivate. Her eyes, these days, darted and searched and stared. The planet didn't offer enough stimulus. And with her delight, she seemed to communicate, How come you can't do all that? Why not that? There's the money, you dope. There's the steady life. Look at this Benjamin Williams. Look how easy. Look how he's landed, midstride, atop this spinning planet. And with calm on his face, as though he'd never known a day of trouble. Why not you? she seemed to want to know. H felt like telling the girl to keep quiet, though she never cried and only ever behaved.

Together, they sat and watched Benjamin Williams work until H became aware of dust lifting from the job site, creating a haze. Mud caked to men's boots. Empty coffee cups skittered through the lot. This place was disgusting, and he told Jo so. "This place is disgusting," he said. "These men are not to be ad-mired. They're perverts, at least one and probably all of them." He kissed his daughter. "*Perverts* is a word you'll learn."

After the assault, H's parents told him nothing. They'd been unable or unwilling to explain what had happened, and instead they'd smiled and evaded and pretended as though silence were an answer. H wouldn't repeat their mistake. He would be honest. H took Jo to his chest and told her all about Benjamin Williams and what he'd done. And he wondered aloud why his parents couldn't do the same. H would have understood. He was twelve during the trial, not an infant. There existed a language for a boy that age about crimes like Williams's. H had heard the words: *rape, alcoholism, drug addiction, depression*. He'd seen R-rated movies, police procedurals, dirty magazines. He and the other kids fought after school, giving each other bloody noses. He'd taken punches and thrown some too. They knew all the curse words: *cocksucker, motherfucker*. They'd told dirty jokes, racist jokes. They'd teased the kid with Down syndrome.

A twelve-year-old didn't react with shock or anger, but compassion. He would have listened. His parents had chosen to tell him nothing, to leave him alone, while they suffered, processed, and then, most cruelly, healed.

H told his own daughter everything. "Benjamin Williams is not who he seems," H said. "This man is guilty. He doesn't belong. If he has this job, it's a mistake, an injustice. Williams didn't wait his turn. He's eating everybody's lunch—yours and mine first of all."

When Jo grew restless, he'd turn her toward the harbor so she could watch the boats creak in. When, soon after, she began to squirm and cry, he'd bring her back to the car. He'd check and change her diaper, toss her mess into a dumpster, lay her in the stroller to sleep, then punch in for work.

Each morning, in an email, came a list of clients and a

set of tasks to perform: buy groceries, pick up dry cleaning, straighten homes. The phone provided an address, then scanned H into a lockbox that contained a house key. He let himself into condos, consulted the lists he'd been sent, and got to work. They'd given him a charge card, and for each client, a budget. "Look for the items on the list," they told him, "but don't ignore sales." "Use the extra money for fresh flowers, a pint of ice cream. Treat clients like a girl you're trying to impress," the training agent had said.

H hadn't worked to impress anyone in years. He hadn't thought about how to please a person since he'd been a child.

Four families had been assigned to H. And though he never met them, he waited on them like a butler. He walked a set of Pomeranians that yipped and hopped and growled at every living thing they passed. He tidied parlors lavished with brick and copper-colored wood and filled with furniture that seemed unused. He cleaned homes that didn't have TVs and dusted libraries that spanned walls. The spines of hardcover books had faded from all the natural light. The patios on these condos enjoyed sunshine twelve hours a day. The roof decks had views of the skyline. H filled refrigerators with cured meats, with organic vegetables he'd never heard of or tasted. He mispronounced the cheeses he ordered at a shop in the basement of a building in the North End. Groceries came packaged in paper that was sealed with gold stickers. They went into oversized, stainless refrigerators that featured photos of little sons and little daughters with blond hair and perfect, round heads—this one a soccer star, that one into the arts. These kids were the offspring of impossibly fit mothers, for whom childbirth must have involved surrogacy. Look at these full heads of hair, those BMWs out front, clean the lenses of the reading glasses on the table next to the leather chair, and pick up the *Wall Street Journal* on the way in the door.

And the pleasure H took in this work—selecting chocolates, picking up tickets from the box office, arranging pillows, scrubbing then drying silverware and plates—shamed him. Jo, little angel, came along each day without fuss. She'd take in the sights and sounds and watch her father work and be quiet and good and fill up with awe as if she understood this wealth and were mesmerized. Pulling on her sucker and breathing through her nose, she watched him and waited. Dad would get to her, she seemed to sense, and therefore, no need to cry. And if and when he was delayed—or forgot, say, a feeding or a naptime—she gifted him her silence, this wry, toothless grin, and he began to understand the girl as a protector.

A life, H thought, could be scraped together. They might make it.

Christine, after all, would return. When she texted, she seemed to beg him to beg her back. And he indulged. He wanted her there as much as she wanted to come. Pettiness and weariness couldn't coexist.

He asked her home, but always she changed the subject: "I've knitted her a hat for next winter." "Can you believe this campaign?" "I'm up to a mile a day without stopping."

He imagined Christine's mother milling around behind her—humming, fluttering through bills or newspapers, vacuuming—the TV always echoing in the background. Her family consumed local news secondhand. It permeated the air around them, entered the bloodstream, and corrupted. Every story of a lost child, every car accident, a shooting four towns over, poisoned drinking water, perverted politicians, this disgrace of a government, asserted itself upon them with urgency: they're coming for you.

"Did you hear?" Christine would want to know. "Can you believe?"

He could, but for her, the news seemed to unveil the world's capacity for tragedy. Swimming pool accidents, choking babies, dogs left in the back seats of cars. She couldn't believe all the misery. "Sad," she would tell him. "Just so impossibly sad."

Her real question, then, went unspoken: When will it happen to us?

And, in response, he had his own: Where did all the air go?

That she wanted him there at her mother's—him and Jo—saddened him. He saw his life laid open before him like a cot in a prison cell.

When he followed Williams to the park to watch the man exercise, H had to hustle to keep pace. Williams moved like an athlete. His arms and shoulders were chiseled. H had worked his entire life to maintain a level of fitness that would keep him on the ice. There had been trainers and diets and regiments and therapies and soreness every morning and pain at night. But Williams seemed engineered differently. His muscles had muscles. His waist was fine, almost dainty. His shoulders seemed made for hoisting planets, as though he were bred part human and part more, the missing link for some future species beyond their own. It all seemed so effortless.

At the jazz club, H would drink his beer and watch Williams abstain, and H would want not just one more, but all of them, all the drinks. He'd want to give Jo to a neighbor. He'd want to leave her in a basket on the steps of the firehouse. The alcohol switched on something in him that he hadn't realized had been off—a pilot light reignited, a parking brake removed. H felt in working order again. Williams never drank more than soda water or cranberry juice or Diet Coke. And even still, that waitress hovered around Williams, pushed her chest up into his face, had only smiles, and batted her eyes and put a hand on his forearm to remind him what a touch could do to the blood. But when she came to H's table, she looked at Jo and said, "How cute," and she left the check for him without asking if he wanted anything more.

Which women did Williams bring home at night? How easy was it for him? All those years away must have made the man ravenous. And H could see that for certain women who didn't know better, Williams might seem right: quiet, polite, fit. The man had freedom that H never had. He had options. And H had a child, a girlfriend who lived with her mother, a shit job, a narrow and narrowing aperture through which to watch all other possibilities diminish. When was the last time H had been laid?

Each morning before work, H watched Williams enter a church with his head bowed, then return again, minutes later, unbent and upright. On certain evenings at that same chapel, men and women and Williams sat inside together and did what? Shared their feelings? Prayed? Forgave one another? H watched from outside and wondered where his acceptance was. Where were his people? Who would hold him high?

Some nights, when the baby slept or when she lay in the other room, H took and held instead the gun. He'd scratch an itch with the barrel. Or, he'd hold the weapon, open the chamber, pull back the hammer, move and touch each part, run his fingers over metal. He'd bought a box of ammunition but had been afraid to load any. He wondered what shooting felt like.

Would the metal, once fired from, retain its shine? Where did one put an infant when one wanted to shoot? He thought of a daycare at a firing range and laughed because, of course, this arrangement must exist. What happened in places like Kentucky or Montana? Who was your congressman? Holding the gun, H felt that it had a perfect weight, was a perfectly weighted object. He'd learned, once, about ergonomics. A hammer is a tool because it fits the hand, because it extends the hand. A bullet fired from a pistol made the hand a mile long, strengthened his fist to be lethal, gave him height, gave him weight, hmm, made him unequivocal, unforgettable. Open up a history book and read about men made large by weapons, men remembered, revered, redeemed, and saved.

At night, waiting for the baby to wake up crying—to cry oneself awake, he thought, must be an experience wrought with terror—H would switch on the television and turn the volume low and take the weapon and watch it and think that he could, with this pistol, sign his name as if with a pen. He could take what he'd been owed. The concept entered his mind as if he'd stepped under a hot shower, and he experienced the idea in his extremities, in the tips of his hair, in his dry, creased hands. Then, crying, the baby came awake.

On a Sunday in May, with an Indian summer scorching the city, H followed Benjamin Williams into his church in Roxbury. Cars idled out front so that grandmothers could be escorted in by children wearing bow ties. Pearls glittered. Men wore double-breasted suits with gold buttons and pants creased sharply from the shins down to the cuffs. Women wore knee-length skirts and patent shoes and stockings that covered their skin. Everyone seemed to know one another. As cars unloaded, families with boys about the same age, with girls whose hair had been braided or ironed flat, embraced one another and squinted and smiled in the sun.

When the crowd cleared and the mass began, H entered and sat in a pew in the back and listened to the piano first, and then a singer, and then a band, and then applause. Benjamin Williams sat alone. H watched the man kneel, stoop his head, nod along to the music and the gospel and the call and response. His faith seemed careless. He didn't seem to know when to stand or what to say. Religion seemed to wriggle from his clutches, like an armful of laundry he couldn't corral, socks dropping on the way to the washer. We just mopped in here, H wanted to say, we mopped, and will you please take off your boots.

And yet, the church celebrated. In ignoring Williams, they embraced him. The choir started as if a ripcord had been pulled. The piano man was a riot. Horns sounded. Drums hammered. Hands clapped. The whole building seemed in motion. A priest stood before them and raised his arms and told of Christ the Redeemer. And the congregation said, "Yes, amen." And Williams, soon, looked up from his boots, and nodded and agreed and said, too, "Amen."

Sitting in church, watching this criminal, listening to the choir, hearing salvation and redemption come showering from this priest, H felt weary. Williams, he thought, keep it to yourself. We're busy. We're freezing to death, starved and bloodthirsty. We've lost our way, and we haven't the time to search. We don't want to hear about your salvation. Could you find some way to shut up about all this heavenly peace you've found?

His row cleared for communion, and H found himself

dragged along with the others in the pew. Walking up to the altar, with the kid strapped to his chest, H felt mauled by old ladies in pink lemonade hats and shouldered blazers. Clattering along in high heels, they gawked at Jo. H had the feeling of driving through a blizzard. And his daughter reveled in the attention they heaped upon her. Are you my mother? she seemed to ask with her big, blinking eyes. And H wanted to shush her, to tell her to be cool, to stay small, to stop being seen. But, of course, she was being quiet, and, of course, the world revolved around Jo. Except for Christine, anybody with eyes saw so. This kid, he thought, this kid is running everything already. He blinked twice to make sure he still existed. He could see her in some years— twenty, twenty-five—on a cell phone in a BMW, buying and selling—what, he didn't know. The vision offered only a vague sense of wealth, of success, of something overcome. Would he be dead by then? He felt certain he would.

H took communion on his tongue. Before Jo's face, the priest made, with a hand, the sign of the cross.

And she responded by spitting her sucker onto the altar and hiccuping and crying out. H scurried after and collected the thing, stood, and then, instinctively, he placed it into his own mouth to clean. Then, he was standing on the altar, facing the congregation, sucking on her pacifier, watching fifty—one hundred—black and brown faces watch him. He stood beneath the cross. The child's cries were in-fucking-human. He wanted to throw the baby forth, to cast her off: Here, if it's so easy, you take her! Instead, he looked at his daughter and thought, We were meant to be a team. He thought, How could you? He said, "Shh, shh, shh." He took the pacifier from his own mouth and gave it to the baby, and she quieted. Then H lowered his head and came from the altar. Eyes from the priest and the choir, from the congregation of women and men, and from Benjamin Williams too, were cast upon them. H squirreled his daughter from the church and out into the morning.

TWELVE

The baby cried, then went quiet. H blinked awake. The clock on the TV told him that he'd put her down thirty minutes ago. She bleated again—this impossible boulder always at the foot of the mountain—and then she was giggling. It occurred to H that she'd outlive him, that that's what he was rooting for. The idea struck him as cruel. H kneaded his eyes with the flats of his palms.

"Okay," he called to her. "Okay, youngster."

He'd been eating when he'd fallen asleep—half of a bagel was still on the coffee table—and he stood and tore loose a bite, and entered the nursery.

Benjamin Williams was there. Benjamin Williams was holding Jo.

Seated in the rocker—work boots, dark jeans, dark hoodie—the man cradled the child to his chest, supporting her head in his palm.

H stopped. Williams was looking at her, and he pursed his lips and clicked his tongue like an auntie might, like a grandmother with a lullaby or a story. The baby watched, big-eyed. Her toothless mouth was a void.

H didn't move.

"Sit down," Williams said, without looking up.

H went mush. He felt sick. He took hold of the doorframe to keep himself upright. Jo was three steps away if only his legs would go. Three steps, he thought, and then?

Williams nodded toward a stool in the corner of the room. "Go ahead."

"Put her—" Air hammered through H's lungs, whomped the language from his throat. "Listen—"

"Sit already," Williams said. "I'm not trying to raise my voice."

H sat. The girl seemed calm. Her eyes watched Williams. She batted a hand in the direction of his nose. H stood again and started to go for her, but Williams turned his shoulder, a bear of a man defending a puck. He could, H saw, twist her arms from their sockets, snap her legs at the knees. H stopped, retreated, and sat.

"I've seen you," Williams said. "You've got that stoop in your walk like you've been laid flat by all the money rushing into this city. Your knees clatter. Your hair doesn't sit combed. You look to me like chewed-up bubble gum hardened between the cobblestones, like racism in a jumbo suit in the corner offices of city hall. You'll be here, Andrew, in this city, on this planet, forever. After the big bomb drops, the cockroaches and you are all that comes scuttling forth.

"Yes," Williams said, nodding. "That's right, isn't it? For how many weeks, now, have I watched you watch me, have I watched you lump around, pushing that stroller, morose as a puppy dog?

I thought maybe you're nobody and everybody. Maybe it's all a coincidence. But then, every time I look up, there you are. The front end of that beat-up Corolla fills my rearview mirror, follows me around like my own shadow. I see your license plate when I go to sleep at night. You are the splinter in my mind, the jagged hook that won't let me loose."

Williams closed his eyes and went silent. And Jo was a speck, there, in his hands, petals falling from a flower, dust motes rising in the sun.

She'd had the gravity of a planet spinning. Every building H had jumped from had led him straight to her. Every door opened into her dressing room. But he'd mistaken her urgency for strength. Curled within Williams's biceps, H saw Jo as she was: fragile. That she'd come into this world and endured occurred to him, finally, as the miracle that it was. Her skin was pale and pink and perfect, against his, which was dark and tattooed at the forearms. He had scars running up both wrists, and she had fingers like jelly beans. She had a heart that beat and grew and moved blood from her toes to her brain to her belly. Benjamin Williams had dirt under his fingernails.

The man opened his eyes.

"You are everywhere," Williams said. "Watching me go, laying out my clothes for me, microwaving my dinner at night. I sneeze, and you bless me and you stare and you tell me to be quiet. There is no leaving you behind, and so, I decide, there is no accident in your presence. We are not college roommates, assigned by lottery. Our kids do not play T-ball together. You're following me. And once I know that, I make a list. I start thinking, To whom do I owe what, and why? My sins, one after the next, line up in my mind, order their chaos for my scrutiny.

Because if you're following me, then who you are must have something to do with what I've done."

Williams touched Jo's nose with a knuckle.

"Of course, there is the one transgression that comes from and leads to all the others, that is the beginning and the end and the beginning again. Don't we all have that one sin? Mine, as you know, is public record, never to be expunged."

H had ignored the girl. She'd grown while H had been watching all the wrong channels. He wanted it over again. He would do better. Didn't Williams see? Couldn't the man understand? Her feet in her socks, her chest, the curve of her knees, were too small. H anticipated a suffering that he could not imagine.

"Who could you be? You're my angel, my jury, my parole officer rolled into one. Do I hate you?" Williams smiled. "Then what? Hate the sound a clock makes as it ticks? As if I had pride left to swallow. I lie down on a couch, Andrew, and I disappear into the fabric."

H felt his muscles as percussion instruments. His pulse thundered. He looked down and saw that both hands were fists. His fingernails were digging into his palms.

He hadn't been breathing. How long? H inhaled.

"I haven't got any money," Williams said. "All my friends are dead or they've blasted off of this planet. The lights switch off whenever I drive by. The zombies have come, and they won't even eat my brains. Or am I the zombie? Am I the scenery? What ever happened to my voice? I want to vote in the next election. I want to shake the hand of my politician. I want to sit in the park and listen to children laugh. Anybody who says hello is always offering me everything. Do I want seconds? Do I want to lie down? Do I want an aspirin, a pill, a drink? Nobody can ever stop wanting to know how I feel. I am the frog pinned open beneath the microscope."

H remembered the gun. God bless Billy, there was the gun.

"People ask how I feel. Exhausted, is the answer. Undeserving. I am a wolf in wolf's clothing. I want that drink. I want that fuck. I have seen both sides of the line, and I belong exactly nowhere. Inaction is not an option. Plates are wobbling, Andrew. The bridge is out, and I am rushing straight toward it. Am I, also, a coward? Is that the only thing left for me to own? Fine then. Fine. I, too, have something to say, Andrew. I've been looking for a volunteer from the audience. I thank you for your service."

The gun was where H had put it: in the drawer of the baby's changing table, just beyond Williams's left shoulder, not eight feet from where he now sat.

"Your kid is cute," Williams said. "I see Sarah in her. Which isn't to say that I see Sarah as cute, but rather, I see her everywhere. I think this is how I'm misunderstood."

Williams smiled, and H thought he could have the pistol in three strides. In a matter of seconds, he would once again have the metal against his skin.

"You aren't one for spy work, Andrew. Do not call up the FBI. Do not, please, commit any crimes. Take it from me. I mean, a baby strapped to your chest." Williams laughed. He had a wide, white smile. "Is there anything more conspicuous than a grown man with a baby dangling from his chest? Especially a cute one like this. Might as well have a harem of middle-aged women following you. Might as well wear a siren around your neck. Still, it took me forever to place you. No offense, but I hadn't thought of you in eleven years, and even then, you barely registered in my mind. That wasn't where my head was at in those days. When I thought about the damage I'd done, I saw only myself. Sarah bore the brunt of the blast; I endured the fallout. Selfish isn't it? Or self-pitying? Are they one and the same?"

The bullets were in the drawer under the lamp, behind a bundle of Jo's socks, in a cardboard box that was blue and white; they were brass in color and pointed, and they were next to her pink and gray and yellow and white cotton clothing.

"When I saw you in that church—standing up on that altar, pacified—I thought, Is there nothing I can't ruin? Will I drag my mess here and there until no sacred place is left unspoiled? At first, I saw Sarah in your face—your nose, your cheekbones—and I thought that's what being outside would mean to me: that I would see her in every stranger that passed, that she would follow me everywhere I went. I thought that that was the punchline.

"But when I saw you in that church, I realized who you are. You're not a dog walker. You're no spook. You're not some man on any bicycle. I am not, in fact, losing my mind. You were following me. You do look like her. You were there, and you would be there, and every day—every fucking day—you would remind me, make sure that I knew and remembered just what I'd done and just what I am. We'd recut that wound, wouldn't we? We'd keep it fresh enough to eat. Isn't that right, Andrew? Don't we know each other after all?"

How easy it would be, H thought. Williams puts down the kid, moves, then H moves, then H has the gun. Then at last he loads it. Then at last his finger goes to the trigger. He would raise an arm and point. Williams would back out of the nursery.

"Here's what's funny," Williams said. "I don't remember. I remember her face, of course, but the face I remember is the one from court: the child in makeup, stone-still and brokenhearted and frightened. And, yes, she does seem like a child to me, now. Now, she does. But, oh boy, what a face. What that face did to me. Eleven years on, and that child still feels like my peer, which is to say, I still feel like a boy."

H could move Williams out into the kitchen. He would close the door between them and his daughter.

"No, what's so funny is that I don't remember. I wasn't lying in court. I wasn't lying in my letters. I cannot remember what happened that night. I'd been drinking too, Andrew. I was a kid too. What I told everyone was what happened. I drank too much. I blacked out. And when I woke up, I felt like some-body'd come after my skull with a baseball bat.

"Did I ask for her permission? Could she have remembered if I did? I am forced to believe—I have no choice but to believe, though I did not want to then, and I do not want to now, though I wished it weren't so—that I am exactly the monster you all say that I am, that I did exactly what you said I did."

Would H feel the sound of the shot? Would it wake the blood in his veins? Did his teeth ache for meat? Could he stand beneath the sound of gunfire as if beneath a rain in the summertime? Would he hear and see and feel a bullet piercing skin like lightning splitting open a tree?

"Do you understand, Andrew? How do you atone for something you cannot imagine yourself capable of? This is not an out-of-body experience, which is what my lawyer thought, which is what my friends thought. A lot of perpetrators, he said, cannot place themselves at the scene. His words, man. His words to me. I was drunk too, Andrew."

The shot would startle the child, but she wouldn't be able to place it as gunfire. She'd never remember what she'd heard. H could see everything before them. He could imagine this action, the afternoons and weeks and months that would follow.

"That's not an excuse. I just want someone to understand what I've been thinking every day since I woke up with that hangover: Just what am I capable of? Just which monster is hidden here"—he tapped two fingers on his chest—"in my soul? My God. Eleven years, one day after the other, and all I can wonder is, What monster? Do you understand?"

And H thought, You're going to put that baby down, and once we start, you're going to beg for it to end. You're going to pray for nothingness.

"Of course, there was the temptation to blame the last eleven years on who I am. I follow the news: frat boys—white ones— doing something like what I did, but worse, and they get a slap on the wrist. They get detention and community service. And I wonder, If I were white, if I didn't come from Roxbury, how might this have gone? What would the sentence have been? Would the sin have seemed forgivable? Might I have been redeemed?"

Shush, Williams, H thought. Quiet up and put my child down. It's time. Here comes an ending. Let's see this through.

"Useless thinking, I know. I put it from my head. Instead, I think that it's hard to have this knowledge of myself and wish for ignorance. Instead, I try to be grateful. Have I been given a gift? I get to know my monstrous self. Lucky me. Those white boys never will. They will eat and drink and buy and steal and rape and lust and sleep, bellies full, consciences clean, and they will go on to become senators and judges. They will never know their monstrous selves. And I do. Thank you, God Almighty in heaven, should you be up there listening at the other end of my prayers. What a kindness you've bestowed upon me in your infinite wisdom.

"And, just in case I should ever get to forgetting what I did, just in case I should ever get to thinking, Time served, prayers proffered, exonerate me of my transgressions, I step out into the daylight, and I can't walk a block without tripping over some person who's already got ideas set about me: people who don't like the way I look, don't like the way I dress, who hold eye contact for too long or not long enough, who cross the street as I come close, who change subway cars. Like they can smell the predator on me. That, too, is an instinct that we pretend, now, out of politeness, that we ought to ignore. It's not correct, we want to say. Don't judge a book by its cover, we tell ourselves. And I want to scream, 'Cross the street! I am a monster! I will eat up all your children!'"

And H thought, Let's get you off to oblivion, Benjamin Williams. Let's erase you from the face of existence. Let's scatter pieces of you everywhere so that they'll have to scrape bits of your matter from the ceiling, the walls, the floorboards. I want them to find you on the inside of my lungs at my own autopsy. I want you vaporized, he thought. I want you expunged.

"These days, I wake up and wonder, Is today the day? Will I drink it all? Will I have her and her and her anyway? Now do I stand up and say something and flex these muscles? I wonder, When does this monster reawaken? It's here, and it wants from me just one more. It wants action, to be fed, and then, I know, it will want to swallow up everything else too.

"But not her," Williams said, looking at Jo. "Not this darling. Let's let her save us, huh, Andrew? Let's let her be our salvation against all odds. What do you think, Andrew? What, I'm dying to know, do you have to say?"

H looked down at his daughter. He and Williams were watching Jo together.

"I don't care," H said. "I'm not listening to you. She isn't yours. Look at yourself, and then look at her. It's not you who she saves."

Williams nodded. "That's what I was thinking too." He stood. "And then"—he laughed—"and then, I thought, Why not ask? Why not see what he thinks? But I guess I already knew. And I guess I should be going. Would it be crass of me to first say I'm sorry? Because I am, Andrew. I'm very sorry. And so on, and so on."

"Just go," H said.

"Yes. That's the idea. Well." Williams held Jo out before him, at eye level, and they two watched one another. Then he leaned forward and put his lips to her forehead in a kiss. H felt fury. And H thought, Okay, right now. Right this very instant. Put my child down and step back.

Williams, then, as if Jo were his own, leaned over the crib and set the girl down.

H stood too. Jo hiccuped. Williams lifted his hands, palms out, and took one step back and toward the door. H moved to the crib. Another step for them each, and Williams was in the doorframe, and H was beside his child. She grinned. Her gums glistened pink. She was perfect.

H turned to see Williams watching them with something like anguish rearranging his face. His brow lifted, and then, without a word, he left the nursery. H darted across the room and took the revolver from the drawer of Jo's changing table. He loaded the weapon and advanced the ammunition, and then, gun in hand, he went after the man.

Benjamin Williams stood in the kitchen with a pistol pointed to his own head.

H cried out for him to stop. Williams fired.

A flash, an incredible deafening blast, filled the room. Everything darkened, dimmed, and then light returned. Pink splattered. Red billowed onto the cabinets and the ceiling. Williams's body folded. His head crashed first into the counter, then into a heap on the floor. Ringing occurred like sound itself, like a physical thing that leaned against H, then softened and subsided. H's head filled with the wails and the hollers and the screaming of his infant child. One of Williams's shoes had come off, and a foot, bare, with a calloused, pink sole, twitched and stirred. The discarded shoe rested overturned, and a hole as small as a dime could be seen worn through the leather.

His own gun still in hand, H scrambled to Williams and arrived on his knees. He was looking for what was left of the— He was looking for something to hold together, some way to reassemble this face: a crater the color of mushed-up raspberries, an eye socket collapsed, an eyeball blunted red and burst, blood now pooling on the floor. H gathered the heap into his lap. The man's hair shimmered on the back of his skull. H felt revolted. He felt he couldn't look. The foot twisted and lurched. H removed his own shirt and tied the fabric around this flesh, around the man's face. Red covered them. H was drenched in blood and holding Billy's pistol. He was holding, H realized, this man with a weapon in his hand. He began to shake.

With his own pale arms and chest now stained, H stood.

He stepped from the body. Jo cried, and H looked at his hands. He released the hammer of the pistol he held in his fist. The other had flung across the room, against the kitchen wall, and had come to rest on the linoleum.

The body fell still. H fumbled into his pocket, where he deposited the gun and from which he withdrew his phone.

Jo cried, and H crouched and dialed the police.

THIRTEEN

The policeman seated him at a desk in a shared office and offered a glass of water, which H refused.

"You should," the man said, and then he stood and went and retrieved a mug. He brought the drink to H. "What do you feel?"

"How?" H asked.

"Sure. Or what."

Smoke had been lifting from Williams's temple, as if a fire burned inside the skull. The skin around the wound had blackened, had charred.

"Is he going to be okay?"

"Drink some, will you?"

H drank, and the water against his tongue seemed to trigger his thirst. He emptied the mug, then brought a wrist across his mouth.

"It was only a pistol. Wasn't it only a pistol?"

"It was a .22-caliber snub nose. A pistol that size won't necessarily create an exit wound, depending on the shot. It's not a particularly powerful weapon."

"It's a gun, though."

"Yes, it's a gun. Lethal, sure, but in terms of ballistics, it's a relatively understated tool."

"Right." H agreed and nodded. He felt inclined to agree. "He looked bad, though. I thought it was bad, but then his foot was moving. I saw that."

"Sometimes a victim can look perfect, almost like nothing's happened." The policeman leaned forward. "But he's gone, son. He's deceased. Any movement you saw was just synapses firing."

H nodded. "Right."

"Why don't you tell me what happened."

"What'd you say your name was?"

"Keating," the guy said. "Detective Jim Keating."

H nodded. "Right. You said that. Do you know who he was?"

Keating folded his hands on the desk before him. "I thought you might know."

H shook his head. "The baby's okay."

The man nodded. "Yes. You gave the baby to your wife. Do you remember?"

"It just happened," H said.

"It did. Just now."

"And she's okay."

"Was there anything wrong with the baby?"

"Is there?" H began to feel a panic tighten on his lungs.

"I'm asking you," the man said.

"There wasn't. There shouldn't be."

"Then she's fine."

"Christine is not my wife."

The man smiled, stood, took H's mug, and refilled it at the cooler. He returned to his seat. "Everybody's okay. We had our medical team look at your daughter. She's fine. You're fine. The blood on your shirt is his. You sat with him, is that correct?"

"Can you do me a favor?" H said.

"Okay."

"Can you tell Christine to go home? Can you tell her that she's supposed to go home?"

"Your girlfriend?"

"Put it just like that: 'You're supposed to go home.' She'll listen if she thinks that it's something she's supposed to do."

"Hang on," Keating said, and then he waved over a uniformed officer. He whispered something, and the woman nodded and went out front. "No problem, Andrew. No problem. Listen, I don't mean to badger you. This is a traumatic thing. I'm sure you want to go home and clean up and be with your family. It's helpful for us to get the details before you process them. Memory is remarkably malleable. Whatever information you can offer today will help us determine what happened before your brain rewrites your understanding of it."

"Do I need a lawyer?"

"You're not in trouble." The policeman offered a sticky smile, from which emerged gray teeth. He cradled a stretch of gum between his left molars. H didn't know any lawyers.

"What's the name of the man we found today in your apartment?" The policeman took a pen from his shirt pocket and flipped open a notebook. "What happened before the incident?"

H had been watching water occupy his mug. Williams, H knew, was the man's name. But when he looked at the detective, who was holding his pen above a blank page in his notebook, H understood that this man and his people did not. And H thought, they can't know. They can't know what I do. They shouldn't imagine what I would have done. They needed to believe, H realized, that he hadn't wanted to murder Benjamin Williams, that he hadn't followed him, that he'd never once thought much about Williams—not really once—since a decade ago. Outside, in the station or somewhere else, Christine and Jo waited. They were waiting for him, and they three could go home together. He should say nothing.

"I didn't know him," H said.

"You don't know the man?"

"I've never seen him before. He's a stranger to me."

The policeman wrote something but said nothing. "Where were you when the gun went off?"

"I was in the room with the baby, with Jo."

"Doing?"

H shook his head. "Do you have kids?"

"I don't."

"You don't do anything with a baby. There's nothing to do. They just lay there and laugh or cry or smash blocks together, and you keep them alive and pass the time by being nearby: sitting, standing, feeding, sleeping."

"Right. You're passing time in the chair?"

"Yes."

"And then?"

"And then I heard a noise." H watched the policeman record his story, and he continued. "I put Jo in her crib, and I found that man in the kitchen with a gun to his head. I shouted something—I think I said to stop, I think I might have sworn—but before I could get to him, he pulled the trigger."

"He didn't say anything?"

H shook his head.

"And you don't know who he is?"

"I don't know him," H said. "I don't recognize him. He was just there. He just turned up."

"He shot himself—"

"Yes."

"—and you went to him."

"I didn't know what else to do."

"Thinking?"

"I wanted to help him. I thought I could help." H felt a pain in the front of his skull. He put his face in his hands, made a vice of his palms, and pressed his temples until he felt relief. "I don't know anything about this stuff. I don't know anything about him or you. Where's my daughter?"

"She's with your wife."

"Who?"

"With Christine. Your daughter is with Christine."

"She's okay?"

"Both are. Andrew, then what? You got up, you walked around. What were you doing?"

"Did I? I want to go home, detective. Can I go home?"

"There's blood in the kitchen, in the bedroom, in the bathroom. There's blood in the nursery."

"Mine?"

"His, Andrew. His blood."

"He wasn't in the nursery."

"No, Andrew."

"No, he wasn't."

"You were in the nursery, Andrew. You walked around

after the incident. You tracked his blood through the apartment. You sat down on the kitchen chair, maybe? You went to wash up?"

"You saw that?"

"We found his blood, Andrew."

"I don't know about that," H said. "I don't know about his blood. Where are the other police officers?"

"Who do you mean?"

"Where are the police officers who were in my apartment?"

"The police are at your home now. The coroner will take the body for autopsy. The team will clear it out of your house, have a look, and make a decision about the cause of death."

"Shooting."

"Yes, but, we'll look at the gun residue and the entry wound angle. We have to demonstrate that it was a suicide. We'll write a report."

"They're in my apartment now?"

"Yes."

"Can they leave? I don't want them there."

"Why not?"

"There's—there's blood everywhere."

"They're used to that sort of thing. Andrew, you've never seen this man before? You don't have any idea who he was or what he was doing in your place?"

"Do you?"

"I'm asking you."

"I don't," H said. "I don't know him."

"Anything at all you can tell us might be helpful."

"No," H said.

"Maybe he's a junkie you've seen around the neighborhood.

Maybe he wandered into the wrong apartment. Maybe he came to rob you and lost his nerve. Do you lock your door when you're home?"

H shook his head. "No. Yes, we lock the door. Anyway, what does it matter?"

"We want to ID him," Keating said. "To understand what happened."

"Just bury him. Just get him out of my kitchen."

"I understand," Keating said. "I understand. Listen—here." He slid a card across the table. "Why don't you call these folks. They're cleaners. They know my deputies, and they'll fix your apartment up like nothing happened. They're professionals."

"They're cops?"

"A cleaning service. They specialize in this kind of thing. Call them. They'll work with us. We'll let them in once we have what we need."

"Evidence?"

"Notes. Details. They're very good. Your house will be returned to you like nothing happened, cleaner than it was before. Where are you going to stay tonight? Can you call somebody to pick you up?"

"I'll walk."

"Call someone. Get some sleep. We'll figure out who he was. It may be hard to believe, but we're going to make sure you feel safe, that you both feel safe. We'll figure this thing out."

"Both?"

"You and your wife."

"Christine."

"Yes."

"And Jo."

"Yes, you, Christine, and the baby." Keating stood and offered a hand, which H took. "Get some sleep. And do me a favor. Pick up your phone if I give you a call."

H nodded. He stood and left the police station.

FOURTEEN

H came before a moving Honda with tinted windows and wheels that shimmered as they spun, and the driver leaned on the horn, then thudded to a halt. On the other side of the windshield, the man's arms helicoptered, and his face went red, and he seemed to H like an animal in a zoo.

Fucking this and fucking that, the guy wanted H to know. He extended one arm and twisted his hand into a fist. And H thought, Yes, please. Let us. For God's sake, for pity's sake, put your vehicle in park and come now.

The little furball that H had been dragging through the Seaport now skittered toward the curb, yelping. If it pissed itself, H wouldn't be surprised. If it combusted into a cloud of fuzz and bows—its sweater feathering to the pavement in its absence—H would think, Oh, of course. But finding the leash didn't stretch so far, the rat-thing scurried back the other way, and then laid down in the street. And H felt terrific sympathy for the creature: Now, there's an idea.

The car horn swelled, then settled like heat or a bad smell.

H felt the noise on his skin. But then the man behind the wheel seemed to tire of making his point, whatever it'd been. He shrugged, then flicked on his blinker and went around. H finished crossing.

Spring had drawn out the street vendors, who hawked watercolor prints of Fenway Park and Faneuil Hall, who sold knitted pot holders or blown-glass vases or herbal, fair-trade tea. Rain from the night before had collected in potholes, had darkened, gathered sediment, and now stood, oil-streaked and stinking. Light radiated from every direction as the sun ricocheted from the glass towers above. A delivery truck, with an open hatch and an empty box, idled across a lane and a half of traffic, blocking a city bus. A cyclist pedaled past, balancing a crate of parcels on his handlebars. Everyone moved blind. Men and women looking at their phones, men and women hopped up on heroin, moved identically, like the walking dead.

A bum sitting on a milk crate outside the 7-Eleven began to vomit. He set his change cup on the sidewalk and covered his mouth with a hand and retched. White bile splattered to the brick, seeped through the spaces between his fingers. Nobody stopped. The man—finished—wiped his palm against the side of a building and retrieved his cup, which he began to shake again. From across the street, H could hear coins rattling. People on phones, under umbrellas, averted their eyes and passed.

H returned the dog to the tower from which he'd extracted it. A black doorman in a black jacket held the door, and H winced. He wanted to tell the man that he didn't live in this building, that the dog wasn't his, that they two—he and this man—were more alike than different. He said nothing. He entered. The inside of the elevator bristled with mirrors, and for the length of the ride up sixteen stories, H looked at the marble floor, which at least muddied his reflection. Inside the apartment—1603—H unclipped the leash, and the dog scurried underneath the couch.

H unloaded the groceries into the refrigerator and cabinets that wafted closed. As instructed, he wrote and left a note: *I went for a walk today. My walker frightened me. He seems to welcome death. I pooed. I pissed.*

Then H kicked off his shoes and went into the bedroom and pulled back the bedspread and climbed under the sheets and slept.

He woke twenty minutes later, unable at first to place where he was. He felt as though he'd been asleep for weeks. His phone was ringing: Christine. He took the call from this stranger's bed and let himself envision this life as his own. This room, this apartment, this dog growling on the other side of the door, the generous mattress beneath him, the ceiling above, the artwork—a splash of green paint on a white canvas, a twist of metal, dried flowers, a pillow the shape and color of a wand of cotton candy—suggested nothing to him but vague, disposable wealth. Were he to offer all this to Christine, to Jo, would they accept? Would this appeal? Would any of it absolve him?

He answered.

"Where are you?" she said. She called him *dear*.

"Working."

"Working where? We want to walk with you. Which rich neighborhood are you traipsing through?"

"You shouldn't."

"Come on now, your girls need some fresh air. We'll drive in. Us three and somebody else's spoiled pup. We'll look like a family. Who's that, with so few cares?"

"I'm not supposed to." H smoothed the bedcovers atop his chest.

"Who's going to say, huh, H? The dog? Jo?" She paused. "Let's have a secret again, you and me."

"It's busy," H said. He could see his image reflected in the screen of the TV mounted before the bed. "It won't feel pleasant. It sounds stupid, but I have to always be moving."

Jo babbled in the background of the call. H felt that he might be sick, and he lurched from the bed and into the bathroom. Across the mirror, the homeowner had written, in black marker, *Fortune favors the bold.*

"We want you back," Christine said. "We won't take no for an answer. Do you understand what that means?"

"I really should be working."

"I finished my swim," she said. "Eleventh in my age group."

"That's good. I'm proud of you."

"There were only seventeen of us, but I finished."

He nodded. "I knew you would. It's a great accomplishment."

"It's nothing," she said. "Anyone could have done it with a little training. But I raised good money. I raised over five hundred dollars. Your coach gave me twenty-five."

"You did great," H said. "I'm sorry I wasn't there."

Silence fell, and the traffic, hundreds of feet below, sounded as if it were in the apartment next door. H thought, They could line these walls with money and the racket would still rattle through.

Christine said, "I can't imagine what it must have been like. But nobody blames you. You understand that, don't you? You understand that of course this wasn't your fault. It was a freak thing. It was totally random. He could have turned up in any kitchen anywhere in the world. But he found ours. What shit luck. But you did exactly what you were supposed to. You kept Jo safe. Jo is safe," she said. "Do you understand? I love you for that."

"Honestly, Christine."

"Marry me," she said.

"I have to go."

"Marry me in a church or at a courthouse. Marry me, and we can start fresh. We can do it this weekend. We can do it today."

"I can't talk right now," he said. "I have to go."

"I'm feeling better," she said. "I'm feeling so much better. I've been talking to someone. A doctor."

"That's good."

"She said that what I was feeling was normal. She said it happens to lots of women. She gave me medicine to help with the anxiety. It'll pass, H. I already feel better."

H nodded again. "I know."

"Please don't hold it against me. Please. I wasn't— I just didn't know."

Now, he realized, she was crying. He could tell by the sound of her voice.

"No, Christine."

"I will feel better. I'll be myself again. I know it."

"You didn't do anything wrong. Do you understand?"

The dog, seeming to have regained its courage, appeared in the bathroom doorway and bared its teeth. H threw a towel at the creature, and it pranced off to hide again under some piece of furniture.

"I need to get going."

"We're a team," she said. "Us two. Us three. Come have dinner with me tonight."

"At your mother's?"

"Anywhere. At Jim's, at Pizza Hut. I don't care."

"Can you do me a favor?"

"Anything," she said.

"Can you not tell my family what happened?"

"Okay."

"Can you not tell Sarah anything about what happened?"

"Of course, H. Whatever you need."

"Thank you," he said. "I don't want to talk about this with them. I don't want to talk about it at all. I'll call you."

"If you don't," Christine said, "I'll call you. I'm not taking no for an answer. Do you understand?"

"Thank you," he said. "I should go."

"Goodbye, H."

He hung up and rummaged through the bathroom drawers until he found the marker. With his fist, he smeared the text on the mirror into a gray smudge and wrote instead, *Riot is the language of the unheard.*

He replaced the pillow, remade the bed, finished stowing the groceries, put out a treat for the mutt, and went.

FIFTEEN

At the funeral, Billy materialized. H was standing apart, on a hill at a distance, where he could watch the Williams family bury their son. They sang. They lowered his casket into the earth. A priest gestured, and men and women and children approached, crouched, took fistfuls of dirt, and dropped them into the grave. A sermon was delivered, which H couldn't hear, but which he understood through slacked shoulders and jaws, nodding heads, and glossy eyes.

And then Billy came, looking mottled, looking like a leak had sprung from his brow and the sweat leaving had withered him down to bones and blossoms of yellow, cancerous material. His teeth seemed nearly black. He wore a baseball cap with a creased brim low over his brow. He announced himself with a cough.

"Now, I knew you weren't bright," Billy said. "We all had a sense of that."

"I don't think I have the strength."

The weather was warm, but Billy wore a ski parka, and he carried his shoulders up around his neck.

"You'd spend hours behind the house stacking up rocks. We'd crack up laughing, watching from the kitchen. You'd come inside, humming to yourself, looking for a pitcher of water or a box full of markers, and we'd say, 'Andrew, what have you been doing out there?' Remember what you'd say?"

"Please, Billy," he said. "It's a funeral."

"Call it a celebration."

"Fuck you."

"Call it good riddance. A funeral for scum is a party. Bon voyage, you little fucker." Billy tipped his hat and chuckled, which became a cough, and then he was doubled over, spasming, hacking. He spat and wiped his chin. "'Building,' you used to say. 'Building what?' we'd ask. 'Cities,' you'd say. Your mom thought, Oh, he's going to be an architect. It was a pile of rocks, H. Poor thing. She had dreams for you until the very end."

H remembered his mother's passing, how she'd spasmed, gasping for oxygen, as her family stood around her hospital bed. He shivered.

"Of all the simple tasks, son. Oldest job in the world, and you found the most royal way to fuck it up. It pains me to ask, but the child, H, is the child okay? Tell me at least she wasn't hurt."

"Jo is with Christine."

"Well, consult a judge for a verdict, but I say good, grand. One parent is caring and responsible, and the other shoots people in the kitchen. Not a hard call there."

"Please don't talk about my daughter."

"You're building," Billy said. He grinned. "What I couldn't figure out—not for the longest time—is what you're doing out here if Williams is going down there. I couldn't figure out how you got away with it. I heard the shot, of course."

H perked up. "Have you been following me?"

"I heard the shot, and I saw the police arrive. And I saw you talking to that big detective, who went inside and came out carrying your baby. You left her in the house, H? You left her inside with the body? What if he'd gotten up?"

"Don't."

"And then, Christine came and took the girl, and she went to you, and you were simply flat, a zero, a complete empty space. And when the detective walked you to his car, he had for you a hand, not his gun or his cuffs. And I couldn't figure it out. Then Christine and the child left, and out came a body, zipped up like the period at the end of a sentence. And I thought, What has happened in there?"

The family began to sing a hymn.

"I'm going to tell them everything," H said. "I'm going to tell them who I am and who he is. I'll tell them what he did, what time he served, how he was changed—because he was, Billy. That's something neither of us thought to consider. Time passes."

"Don't you think they're going to piece all that together?"

"I'm going to tell them that I'd been following him. I'm going to tell them that I hated him, that following him made me hate everything. I'll tell them about the gun and about where and how I got it. I would have done it, Billy. I swear to you, when he was sitting there, that was all I wanted. I looked at him like he was a steak dinner. I was ready to bite his head clean off. Do you understand? Benjamin Williams was a patch of pavement to be steamrolled, was a body I wanted to trample. That's what

I'm going to tell the police. And then I'm going to turn out my wrists and let them give me what I deserve."

Billy took a pinch of snuff from a tin and tucked it in behind his lower lip. He sucked and spat.

"Of course, the first thing I thought was that they didn't know yet. That they were treating this as self-defense. That the man appeared like an intruder, and you played the diligent father, and *pow-pow*."

"I think I'll tell them everything. Isn't that it? I've been thinking that I'll answer every single one of their questions from beginning to middle to end."

"And then, I read in the blotter that it was a suicide. A suicide? I'm wondering, Is my boy H so clever as to make a murder look like suicide? I doubt it, but the kid has surprised before. But then, why would H do that in his own apartment? Why not anywhere else? And finally, it occurs to me. This man, Benjamin Williams, deranged as he was, had one final gift to offer: a front-row seat. He wanted you to see him take his own life."

"I can't sleep through the night," H said. "I'm tired and I'm awake all the time."

"And yet, what luck. Because now, H, we get what we wanted. He got what he wanted, and the police get to shrug about the whole thing. The important thing, H, is that you don't correct them. Let them think he was an intruder. Let them think he found you. Why? Because that's what he did. Twelve years ago, do you think any of us invited that kid here? He just showed up. He came where he wasn't welcome, dragging havoc along with him."

"Wrong," H said. "That's wrong. He didn't just show up. We

came for him. You and me. We followed him, and we pushed him. What does it matter which gun went off?"

Billy started coughing, and when he settled, he said, "I feel nothing but relief. I feel nothing but vindicated. Whatever else you feel, that's on you. And it will pass. You'll come to your senses. That gun I gave you isn't traceable, H, so talk about it or don't. They say, 'Where'd you get it?' You say, 'The gun fairy.' You say it just showed up one day under your pillow—poof, voilà. Or you say, 'My Uncle Billy gifted it to me, Merry Christmas.'"

"I tossed that gun."

"Good, kid."

"I threw it into the Charles."

"That's good."

"You're afraid."

"I don't have a thing left in this world to fear, my boy. Not a thing. I love you."

"Go away."

"I love you, and I want only the best for you. That's all I ever wanted. Think I didn't have the strength?" He curled his index finger twice. "Think I couldn't pull a trigger?"

"Give it to H to do, is that it? That'll put pep in the kid's step, lead in his pencil. That'll make a man of him." He was picturing his daughter's face. "What were we thinking?"

"You've got some hard head, H. Everybody's been trying to talk sense into you for years. Your father, your mother, your sister, me. Do you remember the strings we pulled to get you onto that first premier team? The money they put up for your prep school? The times your mother begged you to take your grades seriously? How many more fistfights did you expect me to watch? How many more years were we supposed to wait?

Think it's easy to stand by as you come apart? I haven't got much time left."

"I was fine before you came along."

"College dropout, minor-league hockey player on the fourth line and falling, driving a cab for a living. You've been burning up for years. That it was Christine you knocked up and not one of the others that came before was some miracle, some grace of God. And now, H, you and I have a bloodline. Would you have me sit and bear witness? I couldn't. I would not."

"Jo has nothing to do with you."

"She has everything to do with me and everything to do with you. Take a deep breath. This is America. We practice manifest destiny here. It's kill or be killed. Think anybody got anywhere by being polite? Welcome. Now, tie up your boots and get to work. That fortune won't make itself, and your daughter—our family—has a mouth to feed today, tomorrow, and for three squares, now until she accepts her diploma on a stage in an auditorium somewhere. Congratulations. You worked a day in your life. Do you ache? Well, why am I not surprised? Dry your eyes and get on living. And for God's sake stop torturing yourself."

"We didn't do a thing wrong—that it, Billy?"

"Did you?"

H looked out at the funeral, at the family, which was now dispersing. The ceremony had ended. "Of course," H said. "Of course we did."

Billy spat a jet of tobacco onto the grass, where it shimmered brown in the sun. "Let time pass," he said. "You're going to look back on this day and remember a beginning." He came forward and patted H twice on the shoulder. "And you're going to remember Uncle Billy was there when it all started. You did good, kid," he said, and then he lifted his jacket collar and left.

H watched the graveyard go empty.

SIXTEEN

From behind a glass partition came the sounds of the police station: phones chirped; officers whispered, laughed; someone was shouting, though the voice reached H muffled; a door slammed; a newscaster, from a TV somewhere, droned. A cop behind a desk at reception clattered on his keyboard. Another came sweeping through the lobby and out to a patrol car that was parked on the sidewalk in front of the building. Her boots, as she passed, squeaked against the plastic tiles. Daylight came in through the window and brightened the lobby but left the rest of the station tinted white by bulbs stretching the length of the drop ceiling.

H's left foot had fallen asleep as he sat, and he shifted his weight and tapped his toes to get his blood going. His hands, elbows, and knees made a triangle, and on the point, on his knuckles, H rested his chin. When Keating came into the lobby, with a sheaf of papers curled under his arm, and beckoned with two fingers, H lurched to his feet and followed.

The man's gun drew H's eye, and he wondered when it'd last been fired, not for training, not to practice, but for its purpose.

And it occurred to H that, leaving war aside, some majority of all shots were fired for sport, for fun. There, the argument had taken shape: not a tool, but a toy. If 99.9 percent of all bullets end up in a target or near one, then how can it be a weapon? A capacity for violence does not declare a violent purpose. Guns don't kill people, etc.

Keating put him at a table in a back room. Seated, H could see a pit of desks, a reception center, a wall of plexiglass, and then, beyond that, the door to the outside, the streetscape, the bagel shop, the pizza place, a bench on the side of the road. Walking away was as simple as crossing an office.

"This okay?" Keating asked of the room.

The cinder block had been painted gray. The carpet had been worn ragged. "Yes."

"Water? Coffee?"

"Yes," H said.

"Both?"

"Coffee, please. Black."

Keating left to fetch the drink, and H placed his face into his hands and breathed.

And when Keating returned and offered one of two mismatched mugs and sat and asked, "So, what?" H told: He knew who Williams was, he'd known what the man had done, that he'd been following him, he'd been watching his life, he'd seen where he lived, worked, prayed, ate, who his people were, what made him lonely, what made him talk and what kept him quiet. They'd spoken. Williams had held the child. He'd been holding H's daughter, and H had had every intention of—in truth, in effect, he *had*—and it didn't matter which gun had fired.

Finished, H felt emptied, and then afraid. This room didn't

belong to him. These people weren't his own. Ink stained the table between them. From a chipped mug, H's coffee steamed. He'd started to sweat cold.

"In the academy," Keating said, at last, "they tell you to consider the totality of circumstances. Have you heard the phrase?"

H hadn't. He watched his coffee and shook his head.

"It means, think through a problem. It asks the detective to consider everything, interrogate everything: what's unusual, what's amiss. When we found that man in your kitchen, we figured, Junkie. We thought he was hopped up. But the guy's a specimen. He's got a creatine addiction, maybe. Maybe steroids. But heroin? We think to run a test. But before we can get the results, we ID the man. He's got a wallet, after all. And then we see that he's in the system, Andrew. We have his prints. Hell, he was hauled into a precinct in this state on the day of his original arrest twelve years ago. I sat across the table from the arresting officer at the Governor's Ball in 2016. How big do you think the world is, son? How dumb did you expect us to be?

"It's no mystery who the guy is. For the record, we got that in a blink. And then, it's not much of a mystery who you are. Now we've got circumstances to unravel. Now this seems strange. 'Nefarious,' one of the guys said. There's no chance the guy just turns up in your kitchen, of all places, to finish his thought. Something's happening. But we look at the entry trajectory of the bullet. We look at the blast debris. You're either brilliant—some kind of brilliant criminal mastermind—or this guy really did shoot himself, because that's what the evidence tells us. The bullet enters around the right mandible and travels up. He's got blast debris on his right hand. There's no question here. He pulled the trigger, and he did it with your baby sleeping in the next room. His prints are all over the house. All over the crib. He'd been sitting in the room with your daughter—did you know that? He'd been sitting there to antagonize you. You and yours."

"That's not it."

"Pestering you. Terrorizing you. As if what happened twelve years ago wasn't enough, the guy comes back for round two. The guy wants to haunt the next generation. The word is *vendetta*, kid."

H was shaking his head. He was shaking his head no. "You're not hearing me," he said. "I started it."

"You started what, son? You did what? Protect your home? Protect your daughter? Let me ask you something: What evidence would convince you?

"So it's like you say. So you'd been following the guy. So you'd had some big, bad ideas about what you might do. This man showing up in your house confirmed, exactly, any suspicion that you had about whether or not he was dangerous. What happened closed the book. Instinct told you to follow him. You intuited danger. You knew he would come back."

"Stop," H said.

"In this building, we refer to that as a gut call, a hunch that pays off. We call that sniffing out the truth. Sometimes—and this is what doesn't get published in the papers—a motherfucker is guilty. Sometimes you just know it. And sometimes when, for one reason or another, the guilty won't take a conviction, you've got to, well, you've got to instigate one. You've got to tip a domino or two. That's justice, son. Real justice, anyway."

H felt lightheaded. The coffee had dehydrated him. When had he last eaten? "He didn't do anything wrong."

"It's a sacrifice—the kind that nobody wants to think about. Because it's messy. Because it's complicated. That feeling

you've got right now in your stomach"—the policeman pointed—"that's real. That sickens. And it cannot be ignored. But it
can be waited out. It can be swallowed. It can be grinned and
beared, can't it?"

"I had a gun," H said. "Do you understand what I'm saying?"

"We found your silly little pistol, Andrew. Please." He leaned
forward. "What dopes do you take us for, Andrew? Huh? What
dopes? You tracked blood up and down that apartment, includ-
ing, son, on the ceiling tile behind which you hid your pistol.
Okay, so we found that too. Are you offering yourself up for
possession of a pistol without a permit? For filing the number
off a gun? That's your only crime here, and that's years. Do you
want them?"

"Years?"

"Years. How about it? How old will your daughter be in three
to five when you get released. Let's do the math. Three to—?"

"Five," H said.

"Bingo. Want them? Think that'll make you feel better?
Think that's justice?"

H dipped his head and closed his eyes. Did he hate this detective? Was he some sort of monster? Or had H conjured this
man—prayed for him—to deliver H from himself? He placed
both palms on the table to have something to hold.

Keating let him sit silent, then he said, "This is simple economics, son, and all you need to do is count." He slurped his
coffee, then dabbed his lips with the back of his fist. "Go home,
Andrew. This case is closed. Nobody but you is looking for an-
swers, and to be honest, you haven't any idea what the right
question is."

"Why?" H said, thinking that was the question. "Why?"

"Why what, son?" The detective smiled. "We take dangerous people off the streets. We protect the innocent. Justice happens bit by bit. One small step forward, you understand? We don't have the time or energy or budget to do anything more." He leaned back in his chair. "I don't even know what you're asking me—what are we even talking about? The bad guy's gone. Roll credits. All right," he said. "I've got work to do. It's time for you to go home."

H thought that maybe someone else, another officer, would care, would hear him out and listen. Maybe there was someone else.

But then Keating stood, unlocked and opened the door, and stepped from the room. He beckoned.

H thought, Maybe someone else, but he stood too, and he followed the policeman's arm and went out into the station and went, then, out and into the street.

SEVENTEEN

The old man had been watching H for twenty minutes.

He wore his hair short, trousers with a cuff and a Harrington jacket, and he sat on a bench with his palms holding his knees. The dogs chased one another through the park, thwacking mulch from beds, trinkets jangling from their collars. The little one antagonized anything larger—a retriever, a bulldog, a fattened squirrel—then clamored back to H and shrank to zero. The man watched. A game of handball started, and the park echoed with the whomp of rubber against concrete and the shouts of the kids watching.

The callouses on H's hands had flattened into knuckles again. The bruising around his eyes had faded. He'd stopped skating, but he'd stopped eating too, and so he'd lost weight. He felt stringy, mealy. In the mornings, he experienced his body, saw his reflection in the mirror, as though they belonged to someone else, some recovering addict, and not himself.

He wondered if these changes would somehow extinguish the person he'd been, if they'd start him anew. But then, there sat this old man, watching.

Another ten minutes passed, then H whistled for the pup, who stopped, looked up, and did nothing. H went for it, but it squirmed off, darted under a bench, and ran until H cornered the thing against the fence and clipped on its leash. The bigger dog came and presented its collar for him.

Both animals in tow, H went to the man and sat on the bench beside him.

"What happens now," H asked.

"They're not yours," the guy said, nodding. "They don't listen to you."

"They're spoiled, but I'm not the one."

The little dog yipped, but then rolled onto its side and began to pant.

"The brothers at the IBEW bought me a mutt. A rescue. 'Won't be able to tell who's saving who,' they said. I didn't much care for the implication."

"You're surviving, is that it?" H said. "You don't need saving?"

"More the opposite. Not enough left in the pan, you know? Might as well push the scraps down the drain."

H nodded. "We can just let it lie."

The man frowned. He rubbed the length of his right eyebrow with the knuckle of his right thumb. "I don't know if I have that in me," he said. "If you could feel the anger in my blood, son, you'd understand. My body won't let me leave it. We Williamses never did suffer any fools."

"That's a misdiagnosis."

The man chewed on his lips. "I'd encourage you to be less delicate."

"I mean to say, calling it foolish is generous."

"No other way to look at it. You're not a mean fellow. You're no devil ascended from below to stalk us here on these streets. You don't have the gravitas. You don't have the worth. No, it must have been some foolishness that got lodged between those ears. I don't know that you seem sensible, wasting your days walking somebody else's dogs around, but a monster? No. A coward, a sheep, a waste of talent, a bully, a damn moron who can't see enough past his own self to know what's good for him. In other words, a fool." The man paused. "Now you've gone and given it to me."

"Can I offer you a piece of advice? Is that indecent?"

"Not as long as it's true," he said.

"Doing nothing's the easiest thing in the world."

The man laughed. "No offense, son, but I detect an ulterior motive. No offense, son, but go fuck yourself."

Misreading the laughter, the little dog flipped onto its back and presented its belly.

"It's not impossible that it's both: true and what I want. Do you hear me?"

"I keep wondering what sort of man he would have made," the guy said. "If I think back on the boy he was—at seven, at nine, eleven—and I think, If none of this business ever happened—if he'd just skipped that party, if he'd just kept on with his grades—who might the boy be today? That's what I can't stop wondering about."

"I didn't make any of his choices for him. Not one."

"You made yours," The guy said, now turning and pointing a finger at H. "Didn't you?"

"I told the truth," H said. "I told the police everything. I'm no criminal. See." He held out his wrists. "I'm still here."

"Tell me, then. Why don't you tell me the truth? Why don't you say it to me?"

"This is over, do you understand?"

"Say it: you acted against a fragile boy. You pushed and prodded and tormented and tortured that boy—my son. Every day he came home paranoid, wired, sobbing. Did you see that from the other side of your spy glasses? Did you hear him begging? 'They're following me, Dad. Everyone knows, Dad. Everyone knows what I am.' Did you hear that? Did you dare to listen to him speak? Did you see the confession he put into every gesture? Do you know anything about how they abused him? Do you even care about the child he'd been and still was?

"No. All you thought was, This young man owes more. I'm owed. You were never going to let him rest. Were you? That boy was never going to rest."

"What he did—"

"He paid for what he did. There's no excusing his mistake. None. But he paid for that. He sat before a jury of his peers." He snorted. "If you can call them that. He took his sentence. Everybody but you understands that. Your sister—"

"Hey."

"Your sister, she understands. You know that, don't you? She wrote him. Did you even care to know that? And what do you do? You come after him. Fool, bully, coward. You go after a weak boy, for what? To get what?"

"I'm armed," H said. "I'm saying it now not as a threat but just to say it. Whatever you have in mind, I could stop it."

"All right."

"I could."

"That's fine," the man said, calming, quieting. "That's what I expect. It's not going to matter to me one way or another how this all comes to an end. We just need to hurry things along so I can stop my mind from eating itself whole."

"I have every right to defend myself, do you understand? Any court would see that. Any jury would take my side."

"I'm not going to go on feeling this feeling." The man slumped back in the bench and watched the other dogs run around their park. "Not going to keep feeling this nothing, no-good feeling. A man who can't even raise a son. An honest man." He turned his hands upward and opened his palms. "A union man. Playing fair wasn't fair enough. Got to play negative fair, unfair the wrong way.

"Sitting here on this bench, watching you, I kept wondering how you did it. How's a regular man like you, a regular boy, find the hatred? I feel the anger—anger is all I feel all day, every day, from when I get up to when I fall asleep in front of the TV—and still I don't understand how to make it into hate."

H almost laughed. "You want my advice? You want to threaten me, then ask me for my advice?"

The man shook his head. "I want to go to sleep. I want a bed and a darkness that feels like eternity. I've been tired since the day I was born. Then this." He looked to the sky, then back down to his shoelaces. "Lord," he said. "One day I hope to make sense of these trials. For now, all I can say is, my poor son. Fuse lit at seventeen, then a decade burning before the boom. What sort of man watches that and shrugs? And does nothing? How could I live with myself?

"I didn't come here for advice," the man said, standing. He had his hat hooked onto his knee, which, in a move, he took, spun, and reset atop his head: a gray driver's cap. The felt flattened onto his crown. "I came here to apologize. I'm not a spiteful man. None of this makes me feel anything but dirty, but more tired, not less. Just—it seems improper to let it all go."

"I'm going to call the police," H said.

The man nodded.

"You come near me again—"

The man looked down the street, and H followed his gaze. He saw brick sidewalks, the sky scrawling across the floor-to-ceiling windows of an office tower, the cobblestone streets. A man in an apron hosed off the stoop before his flower shop. Three young people sat at a table on the sidewalk before a café. A yellow awning, crisp in morning light, cast them a shadow. The streets had wide lanes for buses, for bikes, had trees planted before every other house. The streetlamps approximated gaslights. Men and women, tall and short and round and black and brown and white, collected groceries at a corner market, came forth carrying cloth bags overstuffed with a kaleidoscope of organic fruits. The sky, against all that brick, which had weathered over centuries into something rust-colored and pleasing and smooth, washed blue. Two young women in shorts and T-shirts unloaded kitchen chairs from a moving truck. One drew a thin, tan wrist across her forehead, then dabbed at the hair that had loosened from her ponytail. Above, trees shook from squirrels leaping, from wind passing through leaves.

H snapped his fingers. "Are you listening?"

"I come near you again, I'm dead. I try anything, you kill me. And so on, and so on," the old man said.

"That's right. I see you again—"

"I'm dead. And so on, and so on. Anyway, I'm sorrier than you'll know about all this. This isn't what I want. I wish like hell I got that sense from you. I suppose that's the difference between us if there is one anymore. I suppose I'll hang onto that, try to use that, all the smug victimhood you've got stooping your spine and folding your brow. I'll remember that poor-me look on your face, and then I'll find some way of settling all this, I guess, as she sleeps. Maybe that's the way forward."

"She?"

"They don't say 'an eye for a tooth,' son. It's not 'an eye for a handshake.'"

"Jesus," H said. "Jesus."

The man tipped his hat. "Anyway, let's not be dramatic. It's damned enough as it is."

H was gasping for breath.

"If you do see me again, I don't suspect we'll be talking. So let's just call this so long."

The man gathered his trench coat from his lap, folded it over his arm, and left, a stiff leg turning a hitch in his stride.

EIGHTEEN

At a diner—the Red Hen, in Manchester, New Hampshire—
the counter waitress wanted to know where H was from
and what his name was and how come he was visiting her
place. He ordered more coffee and told her he was passing
through.

"Coming or going?" she asked.

H shrugged. "I'm in the middle of a vanishing act."

She wasn't very young, but she had tattoos in black ink
running up both arms: a birdhouse without a bird, an arrow
pointing toward her palm, part of a verse of a poem he didn't
know. She said he had a kind face.

"I'm in all sorts of trouble," he told her. "I'm about to let
everybody down."

She looked at her watch and said, "Is it already that day of
the week?"

Later, when busing a tray of food, she spilled tepid coffee
onto the counter and the cash register. She called for Emilio, a
dishwasher, who came from the kitchen with a mop.

"Look what you've done," Emilio said.

"My king," she told him, as he cleaned up. Then to H she said, "I'd lose my head without everyone to keep it so."

"Is that what family is?"

"It's certainly not inhospitable."

"Now I'm thinking about my daughter," he said, and then he asked for the check. "Why is it that she turns up everywhere I look just when I'm trying to get away?"

"You ought to go see her."

"I'm bad news," H said. "I'm the plague. I've made the worst kind of mess. Who's my Emilio? If I go to her, what comes with me is every sin of mine, all of my failings. She doesn't get her father without all that too."

"What better can a man offer a child than all his mistakes?" She filled his coffee again. "You got a picture?"

He showed her one Christine had taken before she'd left. H and Jo were playing with toys on the floor of the pediatrician's office. "Isn't it better that I just go poof? Isn't she better off without all my trouble?"

"Seems like it ought to be her choice," the waitress said. On his bill, she wrote *Option 2* and then her phone number. "But in case you were wondering, I live exactly nowhere."

She moved down the counter, topping up coffee and clearing plates, and the ink on her arms became pictures in motion. H paid the bill and tipped the woman. Outside, dawn flared from every surface, from every car and window and from black pavement possessed of morning dew. The Toyota, parked at a bank across the street, was packed full of junk he'd thought they might want: the rest of Christine's clothes and Jo's diapers and toys and books and photos, whatever jewelry was left around the apartment, whatever medication he'd found in the cabinets—Christine's anxiety pills, leftover ear drops, a bottle of painkillers he'd been prescribed after he cracked his ribs—the television, his toothbrush and boots and shampoo, the laptop he used to apply for jobs that never wrote back.

He'd broken the lease and left everything else at the apartment. He'd split during the night and driven off. That place was toxic. It'd been found, which meant that it could be found again. But if H left, then the old man couldn't find him, and then he wouldn't be able to find Jo either. Didn't that track? They didn't share a name. Jo was invisible. Christine didn't exist. They would look like every other mother and baby in Boston. Leaving kept everybody safe. H felt sure of this.

A woman, belly dangling from the hem of her T-shirt, twisted herself over a barrel in the parking lot to search for cans among the garbage. She looked up and came to H and asked for help.

"Got a penny for birthday?" she said.

H shook his head. "I need to go see my daughter."

"Thank you," she said, and then she walked to the next barrel, and then to the next person standing on the street.

H got into his car and drove back to Boston.

———

Christine met him in the driveway with their daughter on her hip, and Jo seemed twice her own size.

"She's a giant," H told Christine. "She's a weed. What have you been feeding her?" He was carrying bags and boxes and backpacks—as much as one trip would allow. The morning sun made mirrors of all the windows, but he saw a curtain upstairs flutter. Even Christine's mother had come to watch him in.

Jo laughed and pressed her palms together. Christine lifted the girl so she could kiss her father's cheek. H felt terrified.

"She wore her best dress," Christine said.

"You two look like angels. This feels like a miracle."

Christine kissed him and kissed his cheek and said hi. She took his chin and pointed his face toward hers, but every stir of motion hijacked his attention. He heard squirrels thinking about jumping. He could smell wind moving. Somewhere down the street, children at the playground cheered. H twitched at their every cry.

"Hey," she told him. "You're shaking."

"Can we go inside? I'm just so happy to be here."

She took him through a subgrade door that opened into a kitchen. "You can put that here," she said about his things, gesturing at a round wooden table. "I'll give you the tour," she said.

She wanted to show him how she'd made a home of the basement: a bed, the crib, a stovetop with two burners, a sink without a disposal, a medium-height fridge. There were cans of soup in the cupboard and boxes of cereal on the counter. A collection of Jo's toys was scattered across a blanket on the carpeted floor. Christine had been using her mother's cable hookup. She had an ironing board folded up behind the couch. Light came in through the windows on the street side.

"There's no view," Christine said, "and the pipes riot whenever Mom flushes a toilet, but the sun comes in early in the morning, and there's a park just down the street."

"You did good."

"Until we get our feet under us," she said. "Just for now."

H nodded. "I'm proud of you."

"Let me help you get the things from the car."

He stopped her. "I'm down a ways," he said. "I couldn't find a spot. Stay put."

"We'll walk with you."

"Stay," H said. "I'll only be a minute."

"Your key is on the table," she pointed.

H took the key and locked the door behind him and looked down the road to the right, down the street to the left. Triple-deckers lined up like stones in a graveyard. A hundred million souls haunted these streets. In every den, at every kitchen table, white families sat and watched cable news and talk shows and played the lottery and smoked cigarettes. They drove sedans with sun-faded paint, worked blue-collar jobs, drank coffee before dawn. He could slip in here and go missing forever like keys in a junk drawer, like a safety pin in a cup of loose change. There were a hundred places to hide and go missing. There were as many ways to be snuck up on.

He checked the doorknob again, which was locked. He checked it again. He walked through the neighbor's yard and over to where he'd parked the car.

The house, run down and lopsided on its foundation, with gray siding and a cinder-block garage, was worth in this market a million or more. The tenants in the attic upstairs paid rent on time and didn't complain that nothing ever got fixed. The street dead-ended into a school. H could imagine a banker someday standing in front of a For Sale sign and seeing salvation, the wife of whom would have impeccable design sense, the architect for whom would recommend gutting the place. Speculators and hipsters and baristas had come thirsty to every shop front and parking lot in the neighborhood. Christine's mother would die on a couch in days or months or years from cigarettes and alcohol. A realtor would lead in parents with milk-white babies. They'd gasp at all the potential.

H knew the sound.

The weather warmed, but the basement stayed cool. Centipedes scurried along the plumbing in the ceiling. Christine kept tissues in boxes on the kitchen counter and on the back of the toilet for squashing. Sometimes when they cooked, the smoke alarm would sound, and her mother would stamp her feet on the floor above to tell them to be quiet. They'd open the windows and wave T-shirts over their heads. Jo would raise her hands to her ears to block out the sound and crinkle her face and cry. H felt time passing. Or was it running out? Was Jo telling him, with her every gesture, just how finite she was?

Thinking he had to get out of the neighborhood, had to become invisible, H quit walking dogs and began driving again for a different company: a competitor with the same idea backed by the same foreign money employing the same immigrants and delinquents. Driving, he existed nowhere. He could circle the city for days and never be seen.

But some nights, he'd go out and find himself drawn toward Williams's neighborhood, toward where the old man had met him in the park. He knew that these two men—one living and one dead—remained in these streets. Or had he imagined them both all along? Had there never been a Williams, a suicide, and so, was there no such thing as this bereaved, deranged father? Maybe he and Christine and Jo were as invisible, as inconsequential, as they'd always seemed. Maybe this was a fantasy he'd cooked up to add interest, to give himself purpose. A dream woke him most nights: that he was meant to be at the rink, that he'd arrive late only to find that he'd forgotten a skate or a helmet, that he'd finally finish dressing exactly in time for the game to end.

H's eyes itched, and his head ached, and his food tasted like paper. He felt the old man in this city like a lash along the cornea, like an ache in the spine that worsened when he relaxed.

Christine had enrolled in nursing school, and on Wednesdays and Saturdays and Sunday mornings and after class, she asked him to marry her. She talked about a ceremony with his family and her friends at a banquet hall in New Hampshire. She said she'd settle for a moment on the steps of the courthouse.

She was knitting a scarf on a one-thousand-degree morning, when she turned to him and said, "I want a piece of paper with our names on it." "Joanna Harrison," Christine would say, "Andrew and Christine and Joanna Harrison."

How could he say no? How should he tell her that he was afraid to put their names into record? Williams was dead and the old man had disappeared, and yet, they both seemed nearby. Any bit of noise, any movement, seemed a risk. He told her to wait until he had a real job. He begged her to let him settle in. And when she said, "Of course, darling, of course we'll wait until you're ready," H felt his failure most acutely. He would tell her to run off if only he knew she could be safe. He didn't have the courage to leave them alone.

H would run searches of their names on the library computer. He found and read all those old clippings. His face still showed up on the team's roster. His record at UMass stood. The archive of the high school newspaper reported on his six-point game. But nothing of Sarah, of Billy, nothing even of Benjamin Williams, no matter how many hours H spent searching.

Still, movement on the street drew his eyes and sent him into a panic: a dog darting through a neighbor's yard, a lawn mower starting, a bicycle whizzing past that he hadn't heard coming. His daughter could barely put Cheerios into her own mouth. She could choke on anything. He'd read about SIDS, about shaken babies, about malnourishment and disease. Christine struggled to squish an insect in a wad of tissue. She couldn't watch a scary movie on TV. They both had cheeks like angels. They had laughter like bells ringing.

Christine's nursing school was a two-year program, which allowed her to intern and collect a salary. She became interested in the job. Some nights she'd come home and kick off her sneakers at the foot of the basement steps and take the child to her chest, sit, and they'd both be asleep before he could click out the lights. He'd gather Christine's bag, take her laundry into the adjacent boiler room, run a wash. He'd make her lunch at night: a turkey sandwich and a small bag of chips. He'd carry the child to the crib. Christine would awaken and walk herself to bed, where H would join her. He'd be up before her in the morning, before her classes or her shift, feeding the baby mushed-up sweet potatoes from a jar.

H stayed close to the task. He looked after the child, who,

at ten months old, had come to fight sleep with fury. She would wail and scream until she collapsed into a heap in the crib. She didn't want the day to end. The world enamored her. She only wanted more. He found himself watching her monitor and sobbing from the other side of the bedroom door. He found clumps of his hair in the drain. His belly looked as though it belonged to some other man, some old man. He creaked when he moved.

During the days, while Christine was out, he did what he could to tire the child: games and exercise, reading and singing, and playing with toys. Sometimes when he couldn't any longer stare at the same set of blocks, when he couldn't reread about the hippos, he took her out to the park. On those days, he would leave first, keeping the child in the stroller just inside the doorway. When he felt convinced that they were alone, he'd retrieve her. They drove to a playground in another town, in Medford, by the river. He never parked his car on their block. He did the shopping in a baseball cap and a hooded sweatshirt. He cut neither his hair nor hers.

All this, he knew, was paranoia, but he felt time running out. He felt a debt coming due. The thought occurred to him that they could go somewhere else and be done with all this, and so he suggested a move to Christine. "Out of this town," he said, "out of this state, somewhere, anywhere or else. I can drive any place."

"Is driving going to be your life's work?"

"We can start over. We can go wherever you like."

"I'm just getting settled," she said. "I'm just finding my place."

What about me? he wanted to tell her. What about your daughter? He said nothing. A certain weariness began to cloud his thoughts, and at times the girl felt like a prop, a muppet, an unknowable organism who, when she screamed and cried, seemed to do so to spite his efforts to care, as if she knew she could hurt him, as if she wanted blood. Whatever do you know? she wailed. Whatever would I want your help for?

And he answered back, Who are you? How did you get here? What happened to that eleven-year-old kid I was?

At some point, this child would grow, and he'd be forced to speak to her. She'd see and understand his example. What a fright. She made big, beautiful eyes and squealed and opened up her mouth. A single tooth had rooted, giving them hell most nights. In the mornings, though, the baby grinned like the eye of a hurricane.

Most nights, after Christine fell asleep, H was tempted to wake Jo and tell her how different things would be for them someday, to tell her his side of the story. Instead, he opened a beer and turned on the TV and watched late-night programming on mute with the subtitles running. If enough time could pass, then his mind might clear and center and settle. The same infomercials sputtered in the dens of every house on the block. This beer was sold at the corner store. He popped a tab and turned up the TV and put his feet up and watched the wall and thought about flying an American flag out front and thought about a lawn mower they should save up for and tried to imagine, maybe, how much might come from their tax returns.

But he couldn't hold a thought in his head. At night, street sounds woke him. A car crash in a TV movie put his pulse into a frenzy. He saw somebody pass by the window, and he got up and went to the street and watched. He heard everything. His hearing had gone canine. He smelled blood in the air. When Jo cried at night, he told her hush, hush, hush. "You're telegraphing us," he'd whisper. "He might hear you." H couldn't go to bed until he'd gotten up and checked the locks and lay down and checked the locks again—to the exterior, to the apartment upstairs. He'd be sitting on the toilet and he'd hear a commotion, and he'd come running before he'd cleaned himself, having to double back when he learned that Christine had only dropped a dish into the sink. She took no action that didn't come attached to a sonic boom. She could never remember to shut anything: drawers, doors, the car. She wanted to eat out on Fridays, and Jo made a scene everywhere they went. She cried from a booth at the pizza place. Neither mother nor child would be silenced. Neither would go invisible. Suddenly they seemed to want the whole world to see them. Spending cash in pockets and a new haircut and their shoes shined up, here came Jo and Christine, sitting atop the center float. On the subway, everyone watched. The baby, the stroller, a backpack full of toys. Nobody stood to offer a seat. All the doors opened at once. People moved down stairs and up escalators. People stood and read magazines, watched their phones. They crossed the street in masses, in heaps.

H read about terrorist threats. He read about manhunts. He watched TV programs about kidnappings and missing children. He learned about FBI protocol. There was an evacuation route that snaked through Somerville down a road that was always mired in traffic. He clocked the drive, then found an alternative that swept faster. This city seemed designed to keep them in. He'd read about townships in Africa. He'd read about parents who looked down for a moment, to check the phone, and gone forever went their youngsters. To where? Use your imagination.

Think of your worst nightmare. The memoirs with overdue library dates stacked up in the back of his car.

———————

Many nights, he couldn't fight the urge to call his sister. He found that he suddenly wanted to hear everything she had to say.

"Do you remember the hell you put us through?" he'd ask, without first saying hello.

"Every day," she said. "I'll never forget."

"What gave you the right to clean up so well? What gave you the right to get your life organized? Who the hell are you to forgive everyone?"

She'd sigh and apologize and say that she loved him. He'd tell her to never speak to him again and hang up. The next night, after Christine and Jo went to sleep, H would call back again.

She always answered. She always listened.

He pestered her. Did she know how he felt? Did she know what it meant to be a kid in that house? Did she understand his hatred? She wanted to. She could only imagine. Yes, she'd known hatred so vile, so fierce, that it gave her migraines. She felt the memory of that hatred like a deformity, like a limp or a finger that she could no longer bend.

"Not good enough," he'd tell her, and then he'd hang up. But always he'd call back, until eventually he came to understand the question he wanted to ask. "What would you do," he said, "to protect those children of yours from the havoc we all know you're capable of?"

"Andrew," she said.

"I want to know."

"It's not in me anymore," she said. "I've grown. I've changed."

"Wrong. False. You're not looking hard enough. You don't remember what you did."

He'd give her the list: the alcohol, the drugs, the screaming, the fighting; locking herself into the bathroom, slapping their parents, stealing the car, their money; going missing for days, coming back bloodied; the silence, which ached worst of all.

She'd let a moment pass. He could hear her breathing.

"What if you were drinking again? What if you got your hands on more pills? What if you couldn't stop, and you couldn't eat, and you hated everything and everyone? How can you be so sure that you can keep all that from Cole and Melissa and Neil?"

"What happened was horrible, H. It was complicated and shitty, and everyone was guilty, and everyone paid. I'll never forget. But anger passes. You see things with different eyes. I've changed."

"And if you wanted that high so bad, if it was there, in front of you, and none of us cared to stop you?"

"I want that high every day," she said. "I want it always. But I'll never use again."

"Bullshit. How can you know? You can't promise a thing."

"My hunger never relents," she said. "But I don't worry about it for an instant. That's how sure I am."

"You'll give. At some point, you'll have to give."

"All that matters now is my children."

"Because they're your bloodline. Because they're your legacy."

"Because I love them, Andrew," she said, as if correcting.

Was there a distinction? He couldn't say. "And us?" H asked. "Didn't you love us?"

"I'm stronger now. I understand the stakes."

"Wrong. You knew the stakes then. You're just more willing now. Why don't you be honest with me for once and tell me what we both know is true?"

"I'd do whatever it takes," she said. "I would literally do anything to protect my children from me."

At this, H felt satiated. He told her to never speak to him again. He hung up and clicked off the light of the old lady's garage and went back into their basement apartment and turned on midnight TV.

Days or maybe weeks later, color flushed Christine's cheeks. Her energy seemed boundless. And she picked out a ring, which she paid for, on her own. She talked about another baby. She asked him why he couldn't sleep. Putting her palm to his stubble, she said how blessed they were. "Take your time," she told him. She knew friends and friends' husbands who had work they found gratifying. She didn't nag or heckle.

At night, he lay awake and looked at the ceiling and saw two men, both named Williams: a father and his son. H could not forget how that head had collapsed, how the body had fallen to the counter, how he'd bled as H waited for the police to come. It had taken seventeen minutes, time that reoccurred to him with violence. He'd left Jo alone while he waited. The memory made his brow sweat and his skin tingle. Any disaster might have happened. Any other course would have been smarter.

Most nights, he came from their bed hot. H got up and put on the television to quiet his thoughts. He couldn't stop his mind from going. Would it happen? If so, when? If so, why wait? If so, was there anything that H could do to stop it?

On the TV, a man wanted H to buy a powerful cleaning agent, a whitening bleach with a fabric softener. There was a live studio audience. They applauded and out came the pitchman's teeth, themselves seeming whitened under the lights of the camera. "Buy now," the pitchman said. "Two for one! Buy now! You won't believe this deal!" H wrapped himself in a blanket and watched.

NINETEEN

Somebody had set a metal and tar paper ramp atop the front stoop, and Billy answered the door in a wheelchair.

"You're late," Billy said.

"What's all this?" H gestured at the chair.

Billy took a white envelope from his pocket. "What's all this?" he said, flapping the paperwork. "Get my coat, will you?"

H retrieved a windbreaker from the rack.

"Just put it here," Billy said, patting his lap, and H did. Then Billy wheeled himself to the edge of the ramp. Momentum drew him down the steps. "Mush," he said, as the chair rolled. To H he said, "Pull that door closed behind you."

"Lock it?"

"There's nothing in there worth taking." He wheeled himself to the back seat of the car and waited.

"You're not sitting there."

"H."

"Billy, you're sitting up front." H opened the passenger door. "Need a lift?"

"You got a real problem," Billy said. "A real attitude problem." He stood and helped himself into the passenger seat. "Get my chair."

H folded the chair and placed it in the trunk. "Did a doctor give you this?"

When he came back around, Billy had angled the rearview mirror so he could watch Jo in her car seat. She'd fallen asleep on the drive over. "Jesus, those thighs."

"Come on," H said.

"Lord."

They drove north. Billy only watched the girl sleep and said nothing. H didn't want to talk either, so they went in silence. They took 3 to 95 to 3 again. In an hour, they were in Nashua. H exited onto a strip with a Burger King, a Dunkin' Donuts, and a Holiday Inn. Cars lined up three across at every intersection: four-wheelers, beat-up SUVs hauling ATVs, hauling nothing. Political stickers, white and red, spewing anger and designed to enrage, speckled bumpers like blood spatter. Exhaust curled from every tailpipe. The car tasted like air conditioning. The sun beat through the windshield.

At the turn, H went left, then around and behind a chicken processing plant. There, next to a set of railroad tracks, he found a flat, cinder-block structure painted white, blue, and red. He parked beside a truck that had a ladder roped to slats above its bed. An old man came riding in on a bicycle, dismounted, set the kickstand, and began fussing with a duffel he'd tethered to the cargo rack.

Jo was quiet. H retrieved and unfolded Billy's chair, and the old man lowered himself into position. H unlatched the car seat.

"Need a push?"

"I've got arms," Billy said.

Wind swelled, and plastic trash swept out from underneath the bed of an antique Chevy, lifted, and circled through the lot. A kid smoking a cigarette snatched and trapped the rubbish with his boot. He kept his hands in his pockets and seemed to watch the barbed-wire fence stir in the breeze.

Was there a bite to the weather, already? Was that autumn that H smelled? His daughter slept. Billy kept the jacket folded on his lap. He was gnawing on his cheek as he wheeled himself toward the entrance. The guy with the bike said hello. His beard bobbed as he nodded, and then he held the door and stepped aside as though Billy were a cripple rolling through.

Inside, behind the register, a kid with a shaved head wore a baseball cap high up on his brow. A man and his wife and his two daughters selected ice cream from a vending machine. One of the clerks told another to get off his fucking phone and mind the customers.

"I made an appointment," H said.

"Name?"

"Andrew Harrison."

"Did you bring your own weapon?"

H shook his head and gave the kid the white envelope.

"I'm looking to buy," H said. "Here's my waiver. Here's my permit. I want to try something today and make a purchase."

The kid behind the counter nodded. "Okay, all right. What are you interested in?"

"I couldn't say."

"Beginner?"

"This is my first time shooting," H said.

"Are you looking for something for sport?"

"Protection."

The kid nodded again. "Over here." He waved. "Come this way."

H was led to another counter. Through a glass window, he saw an indoor range. The kid drew keys from his belt and unlocked the case before him.

"You're going to want to treat this as if it's loaded. Don't point it at anyone. Don't put your finger on the trigger." He withdrew a black pistol about six inches in length. "What you'll like about this machine is its simplicity. First of all, there are fewer moving parts, fewer things to manage. It's not a double pump trigger, for instance. The barrel is full length, which makes pointing and aiming easy. You're not worried about concealing it, so we don't need to sacrifice size, and the size will help manage recoil. Here."

He offered H the gun.

"What is it?"

"This is two hundred-plus years of American ingenuity. It's a Colt 1911 Classic. Here."

"Can I try it?"

"We can't let you shoot if you're alone. It's a safety thing." The clerk looked at Jo's carrier. "She doesn't count."

"I brought him," H said, pointing to Billy.

The clerk looked surprised. "I thought you two just came in at the same time."

"Can't you see the family resemblance?" Billy said.

"Take her," H said.

Jo was still asleep when H passed her from her car seat to Billy's lap, and her arms, out of instinct, went to him, went around his stomach. Her eyes never opened, and she seemed asleep still when H took the pistol from the clerk.

"How's that?" the kid asked.

"It feels right. It feels familiar."

The clerk nodded.

They led him through a secure door into the range where stood, shooting, three men and one woman: a guy in a Red Sox T-shirt held a policeman's pistol with both hands; a lady in a gray sweater, no more than five feet tall, had affixed her target upside down so she could point and shoot and hit, at shoulder height, the head; the man with the bicycle had three different revolvers on the counter before him; a giant, at least six foot three, took sight down a rifle that looked, in his hands, like a child's toy.

Against the glass, behind H, somebody's children—two kids around ten—watched as their father or their mother or their grandparent pointed and shot and as the targets down at the end of the range shivered from the strike of gunfire.

"This is live," an instructor was telling H. "This is a live weapon with live rounds. Point it always down or at a target or away." Behind him, a man pushed a wide, flat broom over the painted concrete floor. Discarded shells tinkled and skipped as they were swept along, chimed almost like Christmas bells. Around H, gunshots snapped like snares. And they seemed, from this side of the earmuffs, somehow gentle, surreal, as they pattered, popped, like *rat-tat-tat*, like little balloons burst, but the birthday party goes on. *Pop, pow, pop*, and here comes the cake. Each of the targets were black or white—faceless black men or faceless white ones—as easy to aim for as a tree stump might be, their shoulders and heads with no ears and no eyes, but only circles that said point here and shoot.

The pistol had been laid out by the clerk on a shelf before H. He turned. Billy had both of Jo's hands in his own. She'd awakened, and she stood and held his fingers in her fists, and Billy's eyes looked like pure romance for this angel, as if in her he saw a lineage, a line of history stretching from today on, a second chance and Christ the Redeemer. Her eyes, H could see through the glass, were heavy, and they shimmered, as she wondered where she was, as she wondered who Billy was. Her hair had matted where she'd slept. Billy offered her a potato chip from a bag he'd gotten at the vending machine. She took the food and ate.

Jo had grown. She was growing. She'd be someone altogether new in an hour, by tomorrow. H hadn't any idea what she'd say when she learned, at last, to speak, how she'd love and hate, or from where she'd draw her fury and how she'd express her ideas and what she would regret and who she would romance and what joy and sadness this world would give to her. God, it was all right there for them, on the other side of that glass. For any inch of this experience, he would do anything.

H took the pistol and pointed and squeezed the trigger, and the gun fired.

———————

Most nights, H woke not long after falling asleep. Alert, heart hammering, he thought it must already be morning. He felt late or lost. His brow was damp and the basement bedroom, with only its one sunken window, offered no light, nothing to orient him. He turned and collected his phone and saw that not even an hour had passed since he'd closed his eyes.

Christine slept next to him. Careful not to wake her, he stood, stepped into a pair of sweatpants, and checked on his daughter. Jo slept, these days, through until morning. Her eye-lashes seemed half her face. She sucked on her index finger, bubbled forth with a language that only she understood, and was perfect.

On these nights, H closed the door to the bedroom, closed them both in, and then put on the TV, volume low, and sat in the recliner. He retrieved the pistol, and his hand felt once again complete and useful and with purpose. The clink of his wedding ring against the metal pleased him. His fingers found the trigger, found the safety, touched and held them both.

H put the point of the pistol to his temple, pressed the barrel to his forehead at such an angle that a bullet, when fired, would enter and pass through his brain clean, would silence this noise in an instant only. He felt metal against his skin—cold—just as Williams must have, and thought, How simple, how brilliant. A pull of the trigger, the curling of an index finger, and then, an ending.

How much more violence would there be? How many more acts? H couldn't choose *none*. That decision belonged to somebody else. But he could choose *only one more*. That much, H could control. He could choose that this would be the very last. And he could be certain, then, that this final act would be against their people—them—and not his own.

There seemed wisdom in all of this thinking. There seemed peace on the other end. There seemed purpose in seeing it through. H lowered the gun, stood, went to the door, and unlocked the deadbolt. He returned to his chair and sat, brought an afghan up around his knees and chest. He set the pistol in his lap and watched and waited.

The TV flickered and cast light against the windows and

countertops and floors. His wife and baby slept. The room was quiet, and there seemed around him order, a finite and manageable space, four walls that he could see and feel and touch. And H wondered what day it was, what year was this, and who, then, were all our presidents? He could see into the future. He could pick all the winning horses. Step right up, they were going to live forever.

His feet, resting on the recliner before him, seemed weightless, as if they belonged to some other man entirely. H closed his fist around the pistol and waited.

ACKNOWLEDGMENTS

This book has been years in the making, and I'm grateful for the support and generosity of many.

Christopher Vyce has been, from the beginning, a tireless advocate, a thoughtful reader, a shrewd adviser, an optimist, a pragmatist, a champion, and, it pleases me most to say, a kind and generous friend. Every writer should be so lucky to work with a partner like him.

The team at Blackstone Publishing—Lysa Williams, Daniel Ehrenhaft, Josie Woodbridge, Ananda Finwall, Deirdre Curley, and more—could have easily passed on this unknown writer and his first novel. Instead, they've taken a risk, and they've made me feel welcome and supported at every step along the way.

Michael Signorelli asked smart, tough questions that challenged me to defend my ideas and that strengthened this book.

Brendan Hare is as good a reader and as good a writer as I know, and his insights on an early draft set this novel on a better course.

Catherine Con has kept me connected to the wonderful

literary community at Boston University. I'm grateful for all her support and for her own writing, which is always a source of inspiration.

Detective John Cardone taught me how a proper police investigation might go, which allowed me to take creative license and invent some of the drama in this book.

Along the way, there were teachers who made me feel heard, two of which stand out above the rest: the late Paul Reardon and the late Kim McElaney. I'm lucky to have been one of the countless students they inspired.

I learned to read and write at Boston University, from the brilliant Sigrid Nunez, Xuefei Jin, and Leslie Epstein. Whatever works in this small book is the result of the education they provided.

For as long as I could talk, my brothers, Matthew and Michael, have—with patience and curiosity—listened to and taken seriously and improved any idea I shared.

In the long closet, with the light that came on when the door opened, my parents kept the shelves full of books, and they never once let me believe there was anything I couldn't do. I'm forever grateful.

And you, Allie, have been the word of encouragement, the patient confidant, the steady hand, the first reader, and the one who brings joy. Whatever comes of these pages, or of any others I may write, this life that we're building—through your generosity and kindness and brilliance—is the story.